"I Hate You."

His jaw tensed. "Then I'm no worse off."

She despised giving in. She'd much rather tell him to go straight to hell. But that had never been an option. "Where and when?"

Tate's chest inflated. Battle won.

"At my television studios. Monday at ten. Don't be late." So unforgettable and debonair in that tux. "One more thing."

His kiss was swift, overwhelming—the same skill she remembered, yet strangely so much more. Her mind hurtled back and the years slipped away. In this surreal moment she was Tate's again and, incredibly, nothing else mattered.

Brutal reality—where they were, what she'd done—finally kicked in. Shoving at his rock-hard chest, she managed to break free.

The dimple she'd once adored appeared as he genuinely smiled. He was so damn superior. "Just wanted to let you know how sexy you are when you're mad."

Dear Reader,

Everyone makes mistakes. Forgetting to lock the door. Leaving the roast on too long. Oh, and hands up to those who have fallen in love with the wrong man. In the aftermath, we dust ourselves off and confirm that some valuable lessons have been learned. But what if we fall for him again? And harder the second time.

My heroine in *For Blackmail...or Pleasure* prides herself on her integrity. When the going gets tough, Donna Wilks doesn't make the easy choice—she makes the only choice. However, Donna has two weaknesses, and the most dangerous by far is her charming but arrogant ex.

Tate Bridges knows about mistakes—big mistakes that can never be undone or forgiven. He is determined to save what remains of his family from life's biggest knocks, and he will succeed using any means available...including blackmail.

For Blackmail...or Pleasure explores the gray area between social boundaries and staunch personal commitment. The very nature of moral dilemmas means that issues and judgments are rarely black or white, particularly when love—and last chances—are at stake.

Hope you enjoy!

Best,

Robyn

ROBYN GRADY

FOR BLACKMAIL... OR PLEASURE

Silhouette® Desire

Published by Silhouette Books

America's Publisher of Contemporary Romance

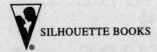

SILHOUETTE BOOKS

ISBN-13: 978-0-373-76860-8
ISBN-10:   0-373-76860-5

FOR BLACKMAIL...OR PLEASURE

Copyright © 2008 by Robyn Grady

Visit Silhouette Books at www.eHarlequin.com

Printed in U.S.A.

Books by Robyn Grady

Silhouette Desire

The Magnate's Marriage Demand #1842
For Blackmail...or Pleasure #1860

ROBYN GRADY

left a fifteen-year career in television production knowing the time was right to pursue her dream of writing
romance. She is thrilled to be an author for the Silhouette
Desire line. She has majors in English literature and
psychology, loves the theater and the beach, and lives
on Australia's glorious Sunshine Coast with her wonderful husband and three adorable daughters. Robyn
loves to hear from her readers! You can contact her at
www.robyngrady.com.

This book is dedicated to my husband,
a gorgeous alpha male—with a conscience.

With thanks to my editor-in-a-million, Melissa Jeglinski.

One

"What a coincidence. Just the person I needed to see."

Donna Wilks recognized the deep, deceptively pleasant voice at her back and choked on a mouthful of champagne. The surrounding black-tie hype vanished from conscious thought. She forgot that tonight was the most important of her career and its success could help so many. As she slowly turned, only one thing registered. Soon she would come face-to-face with her past.

Tate Bridges, Australian broadcasting mogul—the man who had shattered her heart.

Gathering herself, Donna met his eyes and lifted her chin. "I don't believe in coincidence. What are *you* doing here?" She paused to smile at a passing senator then snapped at Tate. "And what the hell do you want with me?"

His darkly handsome face creased in pretended offense. "After five long years? Perhaps a kiss hello is too much to expect—"

She cut him off. "Sorry. I don't have time for this right now."

Tate's casual charm was not only entrancing, it could also be deadly. Whatever lay behind this convenient meeting, it ended now.

As she spun away, her stiletto snagged on the carpet. Gasping, she tipped sideways at the same instant strong arms shot out to catch and reinstate her, front and center. So close, Tate's sensual mouth grinned. His ocean-blue eyes did not.

"If I were you, Donna, I'd make time."

Senator Michaels, a slight and eager man, had circled back.

"Sorry to interrupt." The senator gave Tate a wary glance, pushed silver-framed spectacles up the bump on his nose and spoke to Donna. "Just want to say—fabulous turnout. The ballroom looks spectacular. Tonight's benefit will not only raise Sydney's awareness of your cause, but hopefully plenty of support——" he tapped his back pocket "——precisely where it counts."

As the senator melted back into the animated crowd, Tate glanced indolently around the room. "The senator's right. An impressive turnout for a very worthy cause." He thanked a waiter, accepted his trademark martini and swirled the green olive back and forth. "You always were a crusader. Guess this kind of goal comes with the territory."

Recovered from her near spill, Donna smoothed back a strand of blond hair fallen loose from her chignon. "If you're interested in my efforts to supply more crisis accommodations for abused women, see my assistant." She indicated a bright-eyed brunette who sat with an attentive group by a white baby grand. "April will be more than happy to note your donation."

"Oh, plenty of time for that."

His mouth closed around the olive. Lidded eyes fused to hers, he slowly withdrew the toothpick and leisurely chewed.

A bevy of sparks chased up her legs. Shivering, she ran a damp palm down her black satin sheath and tore her gaze away. He transformed a simple gesture into a deliberate, sensual act so easily. Confident. Sexy.

Way too dangerous.

Only one thing terrified her more than falling for her ex-lover again, and that was defying him.

After his father had passed away, Tate had claimed the title chief executive officer of TCAU16—and it wasn't long before enemies both inside and outside the television network had learned that Tate Bridges was a man neither to refuse nor ignore. After almost a decade winning every big business battle he'd instigated, he'd become known as Australia's Corporate King, though she doubted the title itself impressed him. Tate thought in terms of tangibles, like building, and cementing power in every aspect of his life.

Once she'd been in awe of him. Tonight, for more reasons than one, she wished only to escape.

Skimming a glance over the dazzling evening gowns and crisp dinner suits adorning the ballroom, she stifled a worn-down sigh. "Okay. You have my attention. Can we please just cut to the chase?"

This fund-raiser evening had been organized by the same philanthropic organization that had donated to her project's establishment costs. Every valuable contact she'd ever made was here. She could not afford to waste one moment of networking time.

"I want you to help prevent an injustice."

The muscles in her midsection knotted.

His request was intended to convey a noble slant

as well as a dash of flattery. She might not be able to will away the physical attraction crackling between them, but if he thought she was still that gullible twenty-three-year-old who had hung on his every word, he could guess again.

Her voice was low and laced with indignation. "You think you know me. Appeal to my sense of valor and I'll bow to your bidding."

He raised a brow and sipped his martini.

That same air of entitlement had drawn her to him all those years ago. Nothing attracted her more than a man who was self-possessed—unless it was a man who was self-possessed, built like a power athlete, and made love with a finesse that left her breathless.

The knot in her stomach pulled tighter and Donna dropped her eyes. It hurt to even look at him, let alone remember.

Over the hum of conversation and tinkle of piano keys, the rich timbre of his voice reached out. "My brother appeared in court yesterday."

Understanding dawned, bright and clear. She slowly shook her head. "I should have known your family was behind this. No, I take that back. Libby is a sweetheart. Blade was the one who made bad decisions, and you were always the one to dive in and pull him out."

His eyes narrowed to warning slits. The message was clear: Don't go there.

"Blade's facing assault charges."

The news hit her with the force of a physical blow, but she hid her reaction by setting her glass on a passing waiter's tray. "And what would you like me to do about that?" She shrugged. "Bribe a judge?"

A lock of coal-black hair fell over his brow when he cocked his head, interested to hear more.

Soft fingers of panic closed around her throat. "That was a joke, Tate."

"From the crowd I've seen here tonight, you make some impressive connections. I'm not above a bribe for something this important."

No kidding.

Exasperated, she set off, weaving through the crowd, headed for French doors that opened onto a city-view balcony. She needed air, but more she needed to end this conversation. The sexual sparks were perilous enough; she didn't want government, legal or corporate VIPs overhearing a conversation concerning kickbacks.

Opening the balcony door, she silently cursed. Why tonight, of all nights?

But she knew why. He'd specifically chosen this time and place to put her off balance—to make it easier for him to take control.

Outside, muggy summer heat hit her like a wall, but she persevered and crossed the sandstone tiles to reach a stone pillar entwined with bloodred bougainvillea. Knowing her nemesis would be directly behind, she crossed her arms and turned on her heel.

"I honestly believe you'd stoop to any level to shield your family, no matter what they were guilty of," she told him.

Coming to a stop, Tate braced his long legs shoulder width apart. Sliding one hand into a trouser pocket, he said in all sincerity, "I'm not ashamed to admit it."

Donna told herself not to stare at that broad chest, which looked more than magnificent in a starched dress shirt visible beneath the jacket, or breathe too deeply his masculine sandalwood scent that somehow seemed stronger now they were alone. Instead she thought of how Tate's parents had died nine years ago, leaving him responsible for a rebellious teen and a desperately sad little girl.

She understood his need to protect his siblings, and admired his dedication on a purely emotional level. But she didn't need her psychology degree to see that Tate refused to acknowledge the truth: by constantly bailing Blade out, he was not only condoning bad behavior, in a sense, he was promoting it.

Sometimes tough love was the best love.

Donna rested her shoulder against the cool hard pillar. "The jury came in long ago. You and I aren't on the same page as far as Blade is concerned. But I won't argue now." She needed to get back to her guests.

Not that Tate would care about the project she'd put her heart and soul into these past years. As far as he was concerned, Tate Bridges's priorities were everyone's priorities. Dedication and pride were the very qualities that made him great, as well as so damn arrogant.

Tate placed his glass on a nearby ledge. "As soon as we settle a point, I'll let you get back to appeasing your conscience."

Her blood turned to ice. Brows knitted, she searched his eyes. "Just what is that supposed to mean?"

A flicker of emotion—cynicism perhaps, surely not concern—passed across his eyes. "Let's stay on track. We were discussing my brother's predicament."

He set one palm high on the pillar and, leaning, penned her in. As his gaze traveled to her lips, her breasts tingled beneath her soft cowl neckline and a flood of warmth washed up her neck. He leaned closer and the heat swept south. When she shifted to press her bare back farther away and against the stone, the gleam in his eyes told her he'd noticed and approved.

"I'll ask a question," he said, his breath warm against her lips, "you'll say yes and we'll both be on our way."

As unease warred with mutinous desire, movement beyond Tate's shoulder caught her eye. April, her assistant, appeared at the balcony doors and looked around. Donna slumped with relief. Rescued…for the moment.

Aware of company, Tate reluctantly straightened and eased aside.

Spotting Donna, April waved and approached. She sent a quick curious nod Tate's way before addressing her boss. "Mrs. deWalters is searching for you. You probably shouldn't keep her waiting. I heard her say she has a late dinner appointment and needs to leave soon."

Donna's knees turned to rubber. Oh, Lord. Mrs. deWalters was the one person she promised herself she'd speak with tonight.

She tried her best to smile. "I'll be right in."

As April left, Tate crossed his arms and growled. "Maeve deWalters. I'd have given you more credit than to get tangled up with that old battle-axe."

A history of antagonism and resentment ran wide and deep between the Bridgeses and deWalterses families. Donna knew little about the feud, other than how it had affected Blade and the woman he'd once loved, Kristen deWalters. But that had nothing to do with her.

"Mrs. deWalters has indicated she may be interested in providing significant financial support toward maintenance costs." The Sydney doyen of society might be pretentious and haughty, but Donna wouldn't let that interfere with getting her housing project up and running. "I do not intend to let this opportunity slide."

Tate lowered his arms. "That's your business. Mine is helping Blade. The judge requested a psychological assessment. First thing Monday our barrister will send correspondence requesting your services."

The air left her lungs as the trapdoor swung open. Lord in heaven, she should have seen something like this coming.

She focused on his implacable expression. "Let me get this straight. You want to bribe me into giving your brother a positive assessment in exchange for a donation tonight?"

He hitched up one shoulder then let it drop. "Works for me."

Her hands balled into fists as a scream built in her throat, but training and reason pushed the frustration down. "When will you get it through your head, the world isn't yours to dominate and command? I won't fudge a report. If your brother is innocent of those assault charges, he should have nothing to fear. But if he acted criminally, he needs to acknowledge that and, perhaps, suffer some consequences."

Tate's blue eyes lit with an emotion too cold to be amusement. "So you believe in consequences?"

What a question! "If someone won't admit they have a problem, they're likely to continue to make the same mistakes." Blade was a prime example. Seemed he was still a hothead, in part because he'd been allowed to be.

Tate stood very still. His dominating presence amplified to fill and consume every inch of dimly lit space. "I take it you don't want to help."

Despite it all, her heart went out to him. Tate loved his brother fiercely. She hated to think what he might do to protect Blade, or Libby. But she would not—*could not*—get involved. Much more than professional ethics demanded it.

She tried one last time. "I don't like to see anyone in trouble, but at twenty-eight it's time Blade took responsibility for himself." Last month she'd turned the same age and heaven knows she'd had to work on some issues, half of them stemming back to Tate. But she'd survived. So would Blade. "I will not go against my ethics and act improperly for anyone for any reason." She took a breath then moved to leave. "Now, if you'll excuse me." She'd kept Maeve de-Walters waiting long enough. She was getting back in there *now*.

His voice lowered—dark velvet spilling over rock. "The state board seems to think you already have."

Her blood stopped pumping. He knew about the complaint to the Psychologists Registration Board?

Shifting her feet, she blinked and found her voice. "If you're talking about that ridiculous allegation—"

"Charges of professional misconduct are hardly ridiculous."

The fine hairs on her arms rose at his patronizing tone. The situation was so absurd she shouldn't bother to argue. Surely Tate knew her principles better than most.

"I can't speak in specifics," she began, "but clients with deep issues sometimes experience transference in their therapy."

"Transference...the redirection of a client's feelings from a significant person to their therapist. Often manifested as an erotic attraction."

Something dark shifting behind his eyes told her to tread carefully. She angled her head. "Been studying up on Freud lately?"

"Some psychobabble is bound to rub off when you date a dedicated shrink for a year."

The happiest and most torturous twelve months of her life. After their breakup, she'd felt gutted and hung out to dry for what seemed like forever. Still, she couldn't bring herself to regret her time with Tate. No man compared. But that didn't mean she wanted to travel down that bittersweet road a second time. Not that rekindling of any flames would be an issue.

She got back on topic. "The unfortunate reality is a percentage of clients may believe their therapist returns their intimate feelings then feel betrayed when their affections aren't reciprocated."

"You needn't speak in generalities," Tate informed her. "I've met the man. He's quite convinced of his claim against you."

Donna's mouth went dry. She could barely form a word. "You—you've met?"

"Jack Hennessy showed up on the station's doorstep, demanding to talk to the head man. Said he had a big story and would sell it to the highest bidder, be that my network or one of my rivals. When my subordinate said your name had been mentioned I spoke to Hennessy in person."

Her gut pitched in a sickening roll. "What did you say?"

"I bought the sole rights to his story for an undisclosed amount. My company lawyer confirms that we can present a version that shouldn't result in any subsequent lawsuits. The exclusive is mine to do with as I wish."

"To air to the public?" A cheap shot at the ratings couldn't be Tate's aim. Despite the blinders he'd worn during their relationship, he had never purposely set out to hurt her. In fact, he did his best to protect those he loved.

Of course, *their* love had died long ago.

Tate rubbed his forehead. "My initial objective was to give the guy some sense of power by handing over a big check, then bury the whole ugly mess."

The pressure eased between her shoulders. The relief was so great she could have fainted...but for a single word in Tate's explanation.

She narrowed her eyes. "*Initial* objective."

"Now I'm thinking one hand should wash the other."

A giant alarm bell rattled inside her brain. She assessed his granite expression. So that was his game. Her suspicion had been more than sparked when Tate had mentioned the allegation lodged against her with the Psychologists Registration Board. Now with deadly clarity she realized his earlier remark had been strategic in leading up to this point.

"I would like to propose an exchange," he continued, straightening to his full imposing height. "If you take this assignment and my brother gets the leg up I know he deserves, the story will remain buried." He held up a hand. "And before you spout off about putting faith in the legal system, perhaps we should discuss statistics relating to innocent people sharing cells with criminals who kill to get change for breakfast. Wrongly accused who languish in jail because lawyers and judges and so-called expert witnesses set off domino effects that ruin people's lives. This cock-and-bull charge could result in a twelve-month prison term. Justice will prevail is a great ideal, but I won't take that chance with my own flesh and blood. I intend to stop this sideshow before it has a chance to spiral any more out of control."

Her heart squeezed at the loyalty and stony conviction of his words even as another self-righteous side said nothing justified what he asked.

She set her teeth and shook her head. "No matter how you paint it, this is blackmail." *Give me what I want or face the consequences.*

His blue eyes shone in the moonlight. "A person can only be blackmailed if they have something to hide. If I were you, I'd thank my lucky stars I was the one who bought that exclusive." His tone dropped, low and lethal. "Give Blade a positive assessment, Donna, and get on with your life."

The same chill she'd felt earlier spread like a shroud over her skin. She swallowed against the acrid taste rising in her throat.

"I know how much you love your brother and sister," she ground out. "I took that into consideration whenever you did crazy things in their names. But don't do this. You can't save your family from every fall, Tate, even potentially fatal ones."

The dark slashes of his eyebrows drew together as if he might actually be considering her advice. His eyes probed hers for a long, heartening moment before he rolled back one big shoulder and raised his cleft chin. "I have my priorities."

She glared at him. "And you've let me know once again exactly what they are." As raindrops fell to darken the tiles, she hugged herself and pushed out a breath. "I won't agree to falsify your brother's report. But I will promise to give him a fair assessment."

His lip curled. "I'm not interested in what you think is fair. Given our history, I doubt you'd lose sleep if Blade spent a few months behind bars."

Her back went up. Did he know anything about her? "My job is to help people. I don't want to see anyone go to jail."

"I'm here to make certain that you don't."

He leaned in till his body heat radiated through the thin fabric of her gown and her head swam with the blinding force of his will.

"You won't file a positive report unless you can stand by your words?" He grinned. "So be it. You will spend time enough with Blade to be convinced this was an isolated incident, whether that takes one hour or two hundred."

An isolated incident in a decade full of continuing bad-boy behavior—not likely. Not that she based professional assessments on personal knowledge or background. She was ethical to the core, even when faced with highly unethical situations.

Still, for the moment Tate appeared to have her by the throat. And valuable networking time was slipping by. She needed to get back inside. Mrs. de-Walters wouldn't wait forever and Donna would never get another chance like this to pin her down. Best appease Tate…at least for now.

Reluctantly she nodded. "When's the trial?"

The tension tacking back his broad shoulders appeared to relax a notch. "In two months."

If she couldn't think of a way out of this, Tate would expect her to spend every available moment with his brother until she buckled, which was impossible. Best set some boundaries now.

"I'll see if I have any time free next week."

"Look very hard, Donna, or Maeve deWalters might view a series of stories on sexual misconduct in the therapist world. Of course, if you're innocent, you should have nothing to fear."

How dare he twist her words. Blade's and her situations weren't the same. Even when she was cleared, the scandal invoked by such a story would create such a furore, she'd have a hard time getting anyone to fund her project. Grants could freeze and everything she'd worked for could go up in the smoking ruins of her reputation.

To think she'd almost married this man.

Years of responsible self-healing suddenly came to naught. Her words were a shaky threadbare growl. "I hate you."

His jaw flinched. "Then I'm no worse off."

She despised giving in. She'd much rather tell him to go straight to hell. But that had never been an option. "Where and when?"

Tate's chest inflated. Battle won.

"At my television studios. Monday at ten. Don't be late." So indelible and debonair in that tux, he turned then surprised her by wheeling back. "One more thing."

Before she had time to think, the steel band of his arm gripped her waist.

His kiss was swift, overwhelming, deep—the

same superb rhythm and skill she remembered, yet strangely so much more. With his palm holding her head, memories hurtled back and the years slipped away. In this indefinable surreal moment, she was Tate's again and, incredibly, nothing else mattered. Despite their problems, she'd always felt extraordinarily complete whenever he held her.

Loved her...

Brutal reality—where they were, what she'd done—finally kicked in. Shoving at his rock-hard chest, she squirmed and, lost for breath, managed to break free.

Down his left cheek, the dimple she'd once adored appeared as he genuinely smiled. He was so damn superior.

He turned and crossed to the doors with that casual king-of-all stride. "Just wanted to let you know how sexy you are when you're mad."

Shaking with indignation and insufferable desire, she longed to shout out how arrogant he was. But as Tate disappeared into the ballroom, leaving the doors ajar, the words withered on her tongue. Through the crack, she saw Mrs. deWalters's lime-green velveteen dress headed for the main exit.

Sorting her scrambled brain, Donna pulled herself together. She had to focus and get in there fast.

She darted across the tiles, but thoughts of

Tate—his taste, scent and skill—lingered. Somehow she needed to figure out a way to placate him without jeopardizing her professional integrity. And when this ordeal was over, she would never need to see or, heaven forbid, kiss him again, because that was the last thing she wanted.

Even if her traitorous body whispered otherwise.

Two

Late Monday morning, Tate swept like a hurricane into his spacious top-floor office. Spotting Donna Wilks sitting in the second of three guest chairs, he hesitated before closing the door.

He didn't quite meet her eyes as he loosened his tie and thundered toward his desk. "I was held up."

"Only for an hour and sixteen minutes."

At her unimpressed expression and the light shadows beneath her eyes, Tate's conscience twinged but he pushed the guilt aside. Despite what she thought, he understood everyone's time was precious, including hers. She might look like a break would do her good, but he could bet Donna hadn't had his dog of a day.

Circumstances had changed.

She checked her watch—not the slim gold-bracelet piece he'd given on her twenty-third birthday but a large practical face with a black leather band. He noted her slender arm as he passed. The bracelet suited her mocha-cream complexion far better.

Ignoring the winter-sport sponsorship agreement that needed a signature by noon, he hitched a hip over a desk corner. At the same time, she crossed long shapely legs and laced her hands in the lap of a stylish navy and white-trim dress. He breathed in deep. Damn, she smelled good—like the roses he used to buy her.

"I have an appointment at one," she told him, "so let's get down to business. Will Blade and I speak here?"

Back to reality.

"Blade's not in."

She stared for a long, awkward moment before her face hardened with a humorless grin.

"Now I see how this arrangement will work. You jerk me around from breakfast to dinnertime, and my clients suffer because I can't keep their appointments." She stood, large turquoise-colored eyes more wounded than angry. "I know your priorities are supposed to come before anyone else's, but couldn't you at least have phoned to let me know?"

Despite her plea, and his full-length view of her lithe body, Tate remained cool. "Things were out of control here this morning."

She swept up her slim leather briefcase. "I'd like to sympathize, but your blowout has nothing to do with me."

"Guess again." He slid off the desk and crossed his arms. "A film of Blade's alleged assault has been shown by a rival network as a promo for their six-o'clock news."

Donna dropped back into the chair. "Oh, no."

Needing to work off more energy, Tate crossed to the wall-to-wall window and stared at commuter ferries zigzagging white wash across Sydney Harbor's wide blue bite. "The footage shows Blade lunging at the cameraman to stop him from filming, which, by the way, was pretty much the extent of this so-called assault."

Still, having those images televised up and down the east coast was hardly good for Blade's state of mind, or this network.

He'd appointed Blade hands-on executive pro-ducer of the new current affairs program due to launch in a few weeks. The opposition saw their opportunity to discredit and had slogged a double whammy. Hell, if he'd been them, he might have done the same.

Rotating, he leaned back and braced an arm on either side of the window ledge. "My attorney had the footage pulled off the air. He's uncertain about our chances of having it excluded from court."

Her fine wing-tip eyebrows slanted. "I'm sorry, Tate."

As he took in her flawless even features, framed by a fall of honey-blond hair, an invisible band squeezed his rib cage. That's what got him about Donna every time—what had had him hooked for so long. While she didn't always agree with his methods or opinion, she had a good heart.

But a good heart wasn't enough to convince him that she was capable of giving his brother an impartial assessment. To the contrary, he was almost certain she'd be influenced by the past—one night in particular—and condemn Blade before he'd opened his mouth.

But he possessed the key to turn that negative into a surefire positive. If Donna refused to see Blade and, ultimately, refused to provide a positive assessment, she risked Tate airing Hennessy's potentially damaging story.

Blackmail was an ugly word, but no matter what

it took, he wouldn't let Blade spend even one trumped-up day in jail. After their discussion Saturday night, he held all the cards. Donna wouldn't defy him. Few people did.

She unfolded from the chair again. "You'll let me know when I can meet with Blade."

"Absolutely—let's say this Friday at noon." A nice kickoff to the weekend.

She gave him a weary look that said his audacity in organizing her life appalled her. Then she surprised him by saying, "As it so happens, I'm free all afternoon Friday."

His expression opened up as his arms unraveled. "That's a turnaround."

"This might work better if I give Blade chunks of time, rather than bits and pieces."

"I'm thinking that your choice here relates to the fact that giving Blade bits and pieces is less convenient to your schedule and practice than blocking off an entire afternoon when you can spare one." She'd always been a smart lady. "I can live with that."

She had her own opinion of Blade, but surely if she spent enough time with his brother she would realize this assault charge was an isolated incident, that Blade had been provoked beyond any man's endurance. Once that happened, Tate could come clean. He had no real intention of carrying out his threats. He'd simply played his highest card.

He wished he had a choice—something that didn't flood him with guilt when his guard was down. One day, when Donna had a family, she'd appreciate how strong the impulse to protect one's own could be. God knows it had taken a tragic lesson nine years ago for him to appreciate it.

As she headed for the oak door, he focused on the natural sway of her hips and endless legs that tapered to professional yet exceptionally sexy high heels. His groin flexed as he remembered their recent kiss, the way she'd melted for a full five seconds before self-control dragged her away.

He pressed his thumb to the side of his wistful grin.

He could still smell her fragrance as his mouth had possessed hers for the first time in too long. What he wouldn't give to taste her just once more.

Filing that thought away, he straightened his necktie and crossed to see her out. Moving into his private reception lounge, he witnessed a woman bouncing up on tiptoe, her T-shirt-clad arms flung around Donna's neck.

"What are you doing here?" his sister cried out, finally stepping back. "I haven't seen you in ages!"

Past Donna's shoulder, Libby spotted her rather amused, always indulgent, brother. She marched up and set her fists on her designer-jean hips. "I'm ashamed of you." She whacked his arm. "Why didn't you tell me Donna was visiting?"

As Libby skipped back to the guest of honor, Tate wondered if he'd ever owned such a youthful spring, even at the tender age of twenty-two. Hard to believe this was the same shell of a girl he'd become guardian of after their parents' unexpected deaths. Much of Libby's metamorphosis he attributed to Donna. She'd been best friend, confidante and supportive big sister when Libby had needed it most.

"Are you here on business?" Libby went on, holding both Donna's hands. "Or is this a social call?" Her unusual violet-colored gaze sparkled as it lobbed from Donna to Tate. Shoulders slowly hunching up, she bit her lip. "And maybe I should shut up now."

Enjoying the reunion scene, Tate stepped forward, his face set with a mock-stern look. "Maybe you're right."

Donna didn't seem as prepared to overlook the they-might-be-getting-back-together misunderstanding. Her smile was thin but forgiving. "We're not dating, Libby."

His sister's bottom lip dropped. "You're seeing someone else?"

Tate stopped himself from telling her to pull back; he wanted to hear the answer.

Donna's mouth opened, but words took a moment to flow. "Work takes up pretty much all my time."

Libby scrutinized her. "You don't date at all?"

Donna hesitated. "Not...recently."

Tate's mouth hooked at one side. *Interesting.*

Libby's eyes grew big and bright. "Well, you're not leaving till I get the complete lowdown. What you're up to. Where you're living now." She found Donna's hands again and squeezed. "I've wondered about you so often."

Linking their arms, Libby prepared to lead Donna away, presumably to her office in children's production for one of her famous chocolate-sprinkle lattes that were more ground chocolate than anything else.

But Donna held back. After flicking a considering glance Tate's way, she smiled at Libby. "Can I take a rain check? I'll be back Friday noon. We can catch up then, if you're around."

"Sure, I'll be around." Libby shared a curious look with Tate. "But, Tate, when I asked Blade about our usual end of week meeting, he said you were both locked in for a location shoot in Queensland Friday. Or that's what I thought he rumbled, right before he fumed out of here a couple hours ago."

Tate cursed under his breath—firstly because he didn't want Donna hearing the words *fume* and

Blade in the same sentence, and secondly because he'd completely forgotten the location job when he'd arranged Friday's meeting.

He couldn't defer the location shoot. The deadline to get the show up and running by the start of the new season was already tight. Staff to hire, the show's opening vision to shoot. He couldn't afford any delay.

Donna turned to Tate, the expression on her beautiful face smug. "Guess we'll make it another time."

Tate wondered about the shoot, about Blade, then Donna—those smudges under her eyes—and made a snap decision.

He spoke to Libby. "Isn't your show recording today, sweetheart?"

"Nope. Talent's sick."

"I think I just heard a page for you," he lied, swinging his sister around and patting her on her way.

Over a shoulder, Libby grinned. "I get it. You want a private word before she goes." She stage-whispered to Donna, "One day he'll treat me like a grown-up."

Donna rolled her eyes and laughed. "We can only hope."

As Libby and Donna said their goodbyes, Tate raked a hand through his hair. He hadn't realized quite how much he'd missed the sound of Donna's laughter. Hadn't quite understood how much he'd missed *her,* full stop. He thought he'd gotten over her. Thought she must have gotten over him, too.

When Libby disappeared around the corner, Donna met his eyes. "What did you want to say?"

Her level tone said, *I've wasted enough time.* But her eyes were shuttered as if trying to hide the fact she was affected, too—by Libby's reaction on seeing her again, to a surge of memories the encounter had evoked. So many good times. Admittedly, there'd been some bad ones, too.

As he studied her face, his heart rate sped up.

He'd gotten on with life and put the demise of their year-long love affair down to experience. But now something more than instinct said he should pursue this sexual buzz. Wasn't time supposed to be a great healer?

He cleared his throat and took the plunge. "I want you to come to Queensland on Friday. You can meet with Blade there."

Her face contorted then she almost laughed. "Saturday you came close to ruining my night, today you had me sit and wait for over an hour. Now you're suggesting I jump on a jet and fly away with you to some palm-lined beach." She tapped her temple. "You have rocks in your head."

But perhaps then she recalled the unforgettable vacation they'd shared up north, because she hesitated and provided a flimsy footnote. "Besides, I have a stack of appointments that morning."

"Reschedule."

Her eyes went wide. "You're not serious?"

He turned the tables. "You were the one who suggested giving Blade chunks of time rather than pieces."

Her lips compressed, the same moist rims his tongue had run along two nights ago when he'd insisted she give in to him, then had taken that memorable bonus.

She must have read his mind. "Know your problem, Tate? You push too hard and expect too much."

He rationalized. "You did a paper once on the benefits of assertive behavior."

The magnet that was her body drew him nearer. As he invaded her personal space, her eyes grew glassy. She obviously wanted to leave, but he believed some reckless part of her wanted to stay just as much.

Her lower lip quivered. "I know what you're thinking. You're planning some time management of your own."

That made him think of her watch and whether she'd kept the gold bracelet. She used to take it off and leave it on the bedside table the moment he lowered the lights and slipped his hand over her waist to draw her near.

Edging closer, he shrugged and played dumb. "I'm not sure what you mean."

"While you've got me on your books, you're considering wrangling in a little added value."

He merely smiled. He wouldn't confirm or deny.

She swallowed, but stood her ground. "I'm giving you fair warning...you took me by surprise the other night. I won't let it happen again. Whatever was between us years ago is over, Tate. It's dead."

He nodded sagely then, giving in to his most basic animal need, set a hand on either side of that small waist and pulled her close.

As his mouth slanted over hers, her neck rocked back, she mewled in her throat and her briefcase hit the ground. He scooped his other palm upward to brace her back and took full advantage.

Her parted lips tasted sweeter than any he'd known. The brush of her breasts as he arched over her made his blood race and sizzle. Whether she could help it or not, she had surrendered. He felt it to his bones. Knew it in his heart.

She might hate him, but she wanted him, too.

Their mouths gradually drew apart. Still caressing her, he murmured against her lips, "Okay. We're clear. You won't let it happen again."

Her dreamy, lidded look evaporated like a flash of steam. Her body trembled before she wrenched away. Running both hands down the seams of her dress, she glanced anxiously about her feet and collected her briefcase. When she looked up, she was still short of breath and her voice was tellingly deep.

"You don't play fair. You've *never* played fair. This doesn't change a thing."

He kept a straight face. "If you say so."

Half turned to leave, she pinned him with a look. "Don't patronize me, Tate. I'm a woman, not a child."

He watched her glistening lips move and his insides tugged. His reply was half tease, half apology. "Let me make it up to you." Surely a day in paradise was a good place to start.

Her heart, and cynicism, showed in her eyes. "You can't ever make it up. Not with a trip, not with seduction and certainly not with blackmail."

Tate stared at the empty doorway, which led to and from his personal reception lounge, long after Donna had left—until his secretary, Molly, strolled in, scores of production-cost reports bundled in her arms. Trance broken, he headed toward his office but, needing to make arrangements, made a detour to Molly's desk. Both sets of knuckles resting on the timber, he thought it through.

Fair or unfair didn't come into it. The only rules

he played by were his own. And he always played
to win, whether at work, with family, or a woman.
Yet five years ago he'd let Donna go....

"Molly," he began, certain of his plan, "I need
another return flight booked to Queensland."

Molly removed a pen from her salt-and-pepper
bun and scribbled a note. "Anything else?"

"Three nights' accommodation." He rapped the
timber once and headed for his office. "I'm returning Monday morning."

So was Ms. Wilks.

Three

Four days later, Donna jumped as she heard two familiar male voices drifting up the resort's slate path. Shifting, she set her lime and soda on the sun lounger tray and quickly arranged the sarong over her bright yellow one-piece.

Feeling trapped and, yes, a little intrigued, she'd finally buckled to Tate's "suggestion" that she accompany him to Queensland. She'd even succumbed to temptation and packed a small bag with essentials—sun lotion, bathing suit and matching sarong. However, irrespective of the informal setting, she was here as a professional; she might be lolling by a sparkling palm-fringed pool, but limits applied, and covering up was obviously one of them.

As she flicked the sarong again, making certain to conceal both sun-kissed shins, the men sauntered into sight. In knee-length black shorts and an ocher jersey knit shirt, Blade sat on the lower end of an adjacent sun lounger and chuckled at her state of repose. "Hard life?"

Dressed in tailored chinos and a white dress shirt, sleeves rolled to the forearms, Tate looked slightly more of the part of broadcasting executive on location. Pulling up a deck chair, he trailed a hand through his hair and eyed what he could see of her outfit.

"I take it you've had a relaxing time while we were gone."

Flushing, she looked away. "It's been...pleasant."

While rules didn't strictly apply with regard to client-interview locations, her ethical Richter scale was noticeably shaking. The sooner this getaway was over the better, for personal as much as professional reasons.

The longer she stayed in this relaxed south-seas atmosphere, the more memories taunted her and the more her defenses fell. The less control she had over her rebellious emotions, the more unacceptable physical urges would grip her whenever Tate was near.

A waiter arrived to take drink orders—a dry martini for Tate, a juice for Blade.

Donna sat up taller. Now that the men had their location business out the way, for what it was worth, she and Blade might as well get down to business. But she'd need to be dressed appropriately. Time to collect her clothes and a few belongings from the day locker the concierge had provided.

Somewhere close by, a cell phone peeled out the *Mission: Impossible* tune. Blade reached into his back pocket. His face, similar in complexion and structure to Tate's, pinched as he read the text message. "It's from our baby sister."

The sinews along Tate's bronzed forearms tensed on the chair arms as he shunted forward. "She in trouble?"

"No. But my car is." Blade tossed his phone onto the tray. "I buckled when Libby asked this morning if she could borrow it. That text let me know someone in a parking lot swiped the left side—and not just the paint."

Tate explained to Donna, "Blade has a new Lexus convertible." His eyebrow flexed. "Very smart."

"But now very scratched," Blade ended.

Donna expected Blade to roar. Instead he grinned, raked a hand through his collar-length dark hair and fell back against the length of his lounger.

"Libby is such a little minx," he said. "On Monday she asked for the keys just as I was heading out. I put on my sternest face, said a definite no, and still she came back." The hand resting on his forehead dropped to the sandy ground. "It's my fault. I'm a sucker. We all are where Libby is concerned."

Something clicked and Donna focused more on what he'd said. "Monday morning Libby asked for the keys?"

Blade sat up. "I did my best to make her think I was livid she'd even suggested it. The company provides her with a very nice mid-range BMW. Certainly not as expensive as the Lexus, but you'd think she'd be happy given she rear-ended and darn near totaled her brand-new Merc three months ago. My insurance will go through the roof."

Donna chewed her lip. So that's why Libby had mentioned Blade had been "fuming" that morning. Not because he'd seen that footage, but because he'd manufactured a hard-hearted act when his sister had put on the screws to borrow his new convertible.

She preferred to think of Libby as a minx rather than the introverted teen she'd once known. And, despite everything, she was relieved to witness Blade's sense of humor; they'd barely spoken on the flight up, he'd been so engrossed in paperwork.

But a snapshot of his lighter side wasn't nearly enough. If Blade harbored a real problem with aggression, as the assault charge alleged and past escapades attested to, time with him would reveal it.

The waiter reappeared, tray in hand, and Tate accepted his drink. Blade was reaching when the waiter fumbled and juice splashed and drenched his shirt. Blade jumped up and flicked his wet hand while the waiter bowed and apologized.

Blade patted down the air. "Honestly, it's fine," he told the waiter, who was dabbing the mess with a napkin and muttering in a Latino accent. To stop the fuss, Blade grabbed the hem and yanked the soiled shirt over his head. He shrugged at all three. "I was looking forward to a dip anyway."

The waiter finally backed away, but before Blade moved off toward the pool, he sent her and Tate a lopsided grin. "It's good to see you two finally over your gripes. You always looked great together."

As Blade slipped off his loafers then jogged off to dive in the pool, fire consumed Donna's cheeks and neck. She and Tate were not *together.* Never would be again.

Thankfully, Tate didn't comment except to say, "He's grown into a brother to be proud of."

From what she'd seen just now, a part of her might agree. But her profession required an inquiring, analytical mind as well as discrete data. She couldn't dismiss the possibility that either the phone call or the spilled drink, perhaps both, had been staged to highlight his amicable character. She would put nothing past Tate. Which was precisely why, despite her doubts, she couldn't afford *not* to take his blackmail threat seriously.

As they watched Blade swim the length of the pool, flip, then freestyle back with a relaxed, powerful stroke, Donna's thoughts deepened. "He was such a troubled young man when we knew each other."

Her tummy fluttered. She shouldn't have spoken aloud and for more reasons than one. The past five years had seemed to drag, yet now Tate was here, sitting so close that "when we knew each other" could have been yesterday.

Tate crossed an ankle over the opposite knee. "Blade had good reason to be troubled. He was in love with a girl he wanted to marry. Then her meddling witch of a mother announced Blade wasn't good enough and pushed Kristin to accept another man's proposal." He raised his chin as if only now realizing that of course she already knew the background. "I defy anyone to handle that situation without falling in a heap once or twice."

"Flying completely off the rails" was more like it. "And this assault incident has some connection to

Kristin, I believe." She'd received her official court request and had read the notes on the encounter.

Tate nodded. "Last month, Kristin's husband, a big-shot property dealer in the States, dumped her like yesterday's laundry. For sensationalism's sake, the gossipmongers decided the reason was because Kristin and Blade were having a raging affair. Of course, the media needed a statement. When a reporter and cameraman cornered Blade that day, bombarding him with allegations and questions, Blade swore, shoved the camera out of his face then strode away."

Work had been so intense lately, she hadn't watched the news in weeks. "It must be horrible to worry about stories circulating that simply aren't true."

From his focused expression, Tate didn't make the connection between Blade's situation and her own. Typical.

"Blade handled it well until that jerk of a reporter wanted to know if it was true that Kristin was pregnant with his child and ill because he refused to see her."

The sick ache of disgust formed in Donna's stomach and she groaned. "Where and why do they come up with such things?"

"They take a seed and make it into an oak tree, all for the sake of audience share. In many cases, the media don't report the news—they create it."

She raised an eyebrow. *Tell me about it.*

Donna watched Blade push up out the water. As he swiped a fresh towel from a chair and ruffled his dark hair, a pair of young women in bikinis passed, giggling as they eyed him. Blade didn't appear to notice, but rather moved to stretch out on a lounger, stomach down.

"He seems to have matured," Donna found herself admitting.

Tate's foot dropped from his knee to the ground. "That sounded like a positive assessment."

"Do you ever quit?" The answer, of course, was no.

Another, not so easily answered question came to her mind. "I thought he might be irritated, even angry, when you set this meeting up today." The Blade she remembered hadn't wanted anyone's help.

With an almost sheepish air, Tate rubbed the back of his neck. "I said you asked to see him in a relaxed atmosphere rather than the sterile environment of an office."

The air left her lungs. "You didn't! Blade thinks this was my idea?"

Tate's confidence was back with a vengeance. "He was uncertain when I said you were my choice to do his assessment. But today broke the ice. You've seen him in his true light. He's seen you. Everything's good."

She tried to tamp down the flush of annoyance. "I have a strong feeling he won't be happy when he finds out the truth. No one likes being manipulated, Tate."

Herself included.

"When this is all over, I'll tell him the truth."

Although Donna was miffed, on another level she understood his mind-set. Many parents and guardians were overprotective—some even qualified as controlling. But that kind of dominant behavior could turn around and bite. Case in point, Mrs. deWalters.

She might have believed she acted in her daughter's best interests when she'd forbidden Kristin to marry the man she so obviously loved. But Maeve had mentioned last Saturday evening that she hadn't heard from her only child in years. Which brought to mind another young woman.

"If you're still steering Blade's life, I shudder to think what poor Libby has to put up with." Donna sent him a querulous look. "You let her go on dates, don't you?"

"Only if her homework is done." His poker face dissolved. "Of course I let her date. She's over twenty-one. I couldn't stop her if I wanted to."

"From what I saw Monday, you treat her like a teen in junior high more than a woman in her twenties."

He blinked twice, obviously offended. "She

holds a responsible position at the station. So responsible, in fact, I need to check up regularly to make certain it's not too much."

Donna had to grin.

Her attention drifted to his large hands loosely threaded in his lap and a lick of desire curled in her stomach. She'd loved his hands—the way they looked, the way they had touched her. The way they'd once held her with an intoxicating blend of innate strength and tenderness.

"I know what you're thinking," he said.

Guilty, Donna's wide eyes snapped up.

"But I'm not a dictator," he explained, carrying on their conversation. "I'm their…"

When he paused to find an appropriate word—protector, defender?—Donna supplied one that put the whole conversation in context. "You're their big brother."

The building's afternoon shadow had crept over her. At the contrast in temperature, a shiver danced across her skin. Time to move and change clothes.

Standing, she secured the sarong under her arms then twisted the ends to tie at her nape. She felt Tate's focus upon her the entire time, watching and no doubt wondering about the power surge arcing between them. She couldn't afford to let him know she was wondering, too. If he saw any lapse, any weakening in her resolve, he would show no mercy. The thought of a merciless Tate both worried and, quite frankly, excited her.

After smoothing down the silk batik fabric, she removed her hat and smiled innocently. "So, when's our flight back again?" She assumed it would be sometime early evening, not that a late flight was a problem. Tomorrow was the weekend and because she always kept Mondays free for administrative tasks, she had no appointments until Tuesday. "I'd like to know our time frame before I sit down to speak with Blade."

His eyes were dark and hooded, as if, while she'd been covering up, in his mind he'd been easing the swimsuit off.

Slowly, he got to his feet. "Plenty of time. We'll go for a walk. Not every day you get to stroll through paradise. I spend too much time stuck behind a desk. I'm sure you do, too."

A sexy grin bracketed one corner of his mouth as he held out one large neat hand.

Donna's heart thudded in her chest. She was afraid—scared witless, in fact—that if she accepted, he would take that as a sign she wanted to be kissed again. She was even more afraid that some demented part of her actually wanted him to. Tate Bridges was like a drug—he'd taken an age to cleanse from her system and after another tiny taste, she found herself edgy, craving him all over again.

They'd parted not because he'd cared so much about Blade and Libby, but because he refused to acknowledge how deeply his ambivalence toward her feelings continued to wound her. The night of their engagement party, Tate hadn't arrived because he'd been busy rescuing Blade from a scrap similar to the one he currently faced. It had been the final blow in a series of similar incidents. She could understand that his siblings and network were important to him. But where had their importance as a couple stood, or her individual feelings as his girlfriend and, later, fiancée? Their relationship would never have worked then, just as a repeat performance wouldn't work now—*particularly* now. But clearly Tate had his own ideas.

He didn't merely want to kiss her.

Still, she did need to stretch her legs. Surely she could handle a short stroll. Manufacturing a smile, she nodded. "Sure. A quick walk might be nice." But when she ignored his hand, he took hers anyway.

Her body buzzed and slipped up a gear as his grip, both strong and sensual, conjured up a profound sense of nostalgia. Tate was unique in every sense—a man born to lead and hold his course, no matter the cost. But she didn't need a legend. She needed a partner who truly cared. A man who knew the value of compromise. Unfortunately, Tate could never be that man.

When she tried to tug from his hold, he appeared not to notice and began to walk. Unwilling to cause a scene among the other guests by the pool, there seemed little choice but to go along.

They meandered down a path bordered by rustling bangalow palms. The air was warm but fresh, fragrant with the crush of grevillea, pine and sea salt. Eventually they stopped on the crest of a sandy knoll. Donna gazed out over the cerulean-blue water.

Nothing had changed. The view, the clean ocean scent, the incontestable sense of kismet…all a picture-perfect copy of their last visit to the coast.

Tate's sultry voice didn't break the atmosphere so much as blend with it. "We never talked about that night."

As the deep strum of his words took meaning, she surfaced from her haze and bit down against a sharp stab of regret. She didn't want to talk about that. She knew it was weak, but for just one moment longer she wanted to hold on to the illusion that reflected happier, more naive times.

His thumb circled the back of her hand. "Donna?"

Concentrating on the horizon, she tried to push the question aside. "What night?"

"You know what night."

Despite the humidity, an ice-cold shaft whistled down her spine. Grudgingly she nodded. Yes, she knew—the night of their engagement party. She'd spent every day since trying to obliterate the memories.

"The past is past." Her voice was firm, but she wouldn't look at him. She couldn't handle the complicated soul-to-soul connection they seemed to share even now.

"My delay," he went on, "couldn't be avoided."

Fighting memories, she tried to free her hand again, but he turned, capturing her other hand.

Dropping her chin, she clamped her eyes shut and garnered all the moral strength she felt draining from her limbs. If she tried hard enough, she could hold the vision back. To see that night—to remember—hurt too much.

"I got your messages. I know what happened."

"You didn't return my calls."

Don't look at him. Don't fall into those ocean-blue eyes.

"I returned one." The next morning, when the guests had gone home—her family and their friends who had all been so disappointed for her. Their well-intentioned support had only made it harder.

Donna cringed. Damn it, now she could see their

pitying faces. Could feel the shame eating at her heart. And she remembered, too, when she'd gotten home, that she'd cried till well after dawn. She couldn't bear the crush of those memories. She wanted them gone, buried forever.

She'd loved him so much.

Tate let go one hand to tilt up her chin. His intense gaze searched hers as a pulse beat at the side of his neck. "I needed to speak with you…explain."

This was killing her—all over again.

"We spoke, Tate. There was nothing more to say." A brave smile thinned her lips. "And, it's okay, *really.*"

He'd said he was sorry. She'd said that wasn't enough. How many times had he left her waiting— in restaurants, at her apartment or his, and then later at appointments organized around what was to be their forthcoming wedding? Yes, he was a busy man, but as far as feelings were concerned, he could also be an inconsiderate one. If that was life as his girlfriend and fiancée, she'd made up her mind she didn't want to stick around for life as his wife. After the engagement party, he'd left messages, knocked on her door, pounded once or twice, but she'd remained strong…except for that one heart-wrenching slip.

She stomped on the image.

Until a week ago, she thought she'd successfully wiped her conscience clean of Tate Bridges. She should never have walked with him. Should never have come here today.

She tried again. "There's no need to dredge it up again."

His voice deepened. "What if I want to?"

His persistence should have rankled but, instead, she felt the inappropriate urge to laugh.

"You truly are the most arrogant man I've ever met. You blatantly coerce me into helping your brother. Kiss me when you know you have no right. Now you want to—" exasperated, she threw up her free hand "—I don't know what."

His eyes glistened out from the encroaching shadows. "You know perfectly well what."

He lifted her hand till his mouth pressed upon the back of her wrist. A tingling pleasure spiraled up her arm. Mouth lingering, his tongue looped the sensitive flesh, channeling the raw hunger directly to her core.

His scent enveloped her. As his mouth trailed up her arm, his other hand found the small of her back and urged her in against his hips.

He was hard.

Liking the glorious feel of him way too much, she squirmed. "Tate...don't."

"Because you don't want me to hold you? Don't like the push of me against you?" He pressed more firmly and she bit her lip against a soft cry of need. "I think you do, Donna. I think you like it very much."

She closed her eyes but refused to slant her head and offer her neck as he kissed her shoulder. No one else would ever make her feel like this, as if nothing else existed but grasping passion and the aching need to fill it.

But she had to remember…she had to let him know. "I wanted you to stay out of my life."

His smile brushed her jaw. "That must be why you keep kissing me back."

To prove a point, he claimed her lips again, languidly, as if he could take all the time in the world and still she wouldn't refuse him. With each stroke, the thrill went lower, deeper, till everything she was belonged only to him. She should have felt imprisoned by his power. Instead, Lord help her, she felt released.

As his kiss broke into moist meaningful snatches, lucidity peeped through. They were in the open, making love and building to more dangerous, irreversible things. Yet she couldn't bear to tear away from him. He felt too good.

Her palms fanned his hot, hard chest. She sighed and burned with longing. "I must be mad."

"Yep. Completely gone."

His hand slid in between the folds of her sarong

and she lost her good judgment beneath a twirling blanket of desire. But a remnant of common sense still nagged.

Eyes drifting open, she summoned a frown. "I won't sleep with you, Tate. We're going to fly home and that will be the end of kissing and touching and…"

His fingertip drew a circle above the apex of her thighs. When his touch slid down between, Donna moaned and forgot what she was saying.

How did he do it? With little effort, in so short a time, he made her forget everything and want only him.

He nuzzled that sweet spot just below her earlobe and a luscious gloss of abandon cascaded to her toes.

"I've reserved a bungalow with a spa bath over-looking the waves, just like before."

A delicious throb kicked off at her hub and she dug her fingers into his biceps. All comprehension past the hum of his voice and magic of his touch melted away. What had he said? Something impor-tant. She forced her brain to work.

"You're staying the night?"

"*We're* staying *three* nights."

She heard and, at some level, understood. She should object…definitely would.

Through her swimsuit, he rubbed her *there* and

she leaned toward him. "I'm not. I can't. I…I don't have any clothes."

As his lips grazed hers, she felt his smile. "That won't be a problem."

Four

By the time they returned to the pool area, Donna's face was hot with shame. What a deplorable lack of control. Such an obvious miscalculation of power.

How dim-witted to expect she could show Tate she no longer desired him. The simple truth was, she *did* desire him—ferociously. Another moment and they might have shed their clothes and satisfied each other then and there on the sand.

It wouldn't have been the first time.

But as they walked together side by side now, Tate's hand flexing and squeezing hers while they navigated the shifting crystal-blue pool water,

Donna's stomach somersaulted. Her throat felt thick, and she couldn't stop swallowing. He expected her to succumb, completely and tonight. He wouldn't be pleased to learn that since the last explosive kiss she'd had a change, not so much of heart as of reason.

The bungalow and spa bath were now off-limits, no matter how much her raging hormones begged or Tate and his sizzling caresses tried to persuade her. And she had a foolproof way to achieve her aim.

If she couldn't trust herself or Tate, she would have to put her faith in Blade. Heaven knows what excuse Tate intended to give his brother when they met back here. Or perhaps Blade already knew about Tate's cozy three-day plan.

However, irrespective of what left Tate's mouth she would stick to her guns and, more importantly, stick to Blade's side until they were safely back in Sydney. She would handle tomorrow when tomorrow came. Today she had to escape and Blade's company was her only sure ticket out.

Strange. Five years ago she'd secretly, perhaps selfishly, wished Blade Bridges out of her life; Tate was always rushing off to save his hothead brother from one ill-fated escapade or another. But right now she only wanted to keep Blade close. With him near, she could hardly forget the past and why three days in paradise could only end in misery.

Stopping by the lounger where they'd last seen Blade, Tate glanced around the bobbing palm fronds and massive navy-blue and white sun umbrellas. A few people dotted the sandy perimeter of the pool, one couple chatted at the Balinese-style bar near a trickling rock waterfall, but Blade was nowhere to be seen.

Tate pulled up the waiter who had spilled the juice earlier. "Have you seen my brother?"

Donna tried to see past the main building's floor-to-ceiling tinted windows. Blade, too, had left some belongings in a private locker earlier. Perhaps he'd gone to collect a change of clothes. Or maybe he'd dried off and was enjoying the tinkling chords of the piano she heard wafting out from inside. He had to be here somewhere.

The waiter nodded. "The gentleman left in a hurry. He said I should give you this when you returned." He dug into his pocket and handed over a message written on resort paper.

Donna read over Tate's arm.

Received urgent phone call. Must catch earlier flight. Sorry. Blade.

Donna's world shuddered on its axis. Blade had left.

But as Tate scrunched the note in his fist, her mind jolted back into gear. She had to follow Blade, catch a cab to the airport. And she had to do it now before Tate took her in his arms again.

She spoke to the waiter. "Can you arrange a cab to the airport?"

Before the waiter could reply, Tate, cell phone already to his ear, gripped her wrist.

"No need to jump to conclusions and follow just yet." He cursed and stabbed a button with his thumb. "Blade's not answering." He punched in another number. "I'll get Libby on the phone and—" He focused on his call. "Libby? What's wrong?" He frowned. "Did you call Blade?" He shook his head. "No, not about the scratch on the car."

As the waiter edged away, Donna sighed with relief. Whatever urgent matter had spurred Blade away had nothing to do with Libby. At least she could travel to the airport free from worry over the young woman she'd once thought of as her own sister, and who had come close to being just that through marriage. Some weeks after their breakup, she'd left messages with the Bridges's housekeeper. Apparently Libby had been away overseas on an extended vacation with friends, but she never returned those calls. Donna had assumed Libby had decided not to keep in touch, but after the wonderful reception she'd received at Tate's office the other day, she wondered whether those messages had ever made it into Libby's hands.

Setting her thoughts back on track, Donna tugged to release her arm, but Tate, focused on a third call now, bound her to him, his strong fingers cuffing her wrist with just the right amount of pressure—not tight, but firm. Trying to ignore his heated touch, Donna studied the path leading into the main building...and freedom.

She would simply tell Tate quietly, clearly, that she wanted to catch the next flight home. She glanced up at him—larger than life, exuding magnetism and confidence in any situation—and a convulsive shiver ran through her. How very close she'd come to disaster.

His mouth tight with concern, Tate disconnected and slipped the cell into his trouser pocket. "Nothing's wrong at the station, either. Must be something personal."

If Donna could spare the brain power, she might be concerned, too. But she had her own problems. Best get it over with. "Tate, I know what happened back on the beach must have led you to believe..."

The line etched between Tate's eyebrows eased. He redirected his attention to her and he slowly smiled.

"Ah, yes, our...conversation. I recall something about clothes, or lack thereof." The simmering line of his gaze traveled down her throat, across her tingling breasts. "Right now I'm thinking you're overdressed. We both are."

"If I need to apologize for giving you the wrong impression, I will. But then you should apologize for leading me into this ambush."

He held her gaze for a moment then exhaled, slow and patient. "We need to talk."

"No, we do not." There'd been enough talk. Talk that led to lover's whispers in her ear and forbidden sensations spilling through her body. "We need to leave all this behind, once and for all."

He spoke close to her lips. "What are you so afraid of?"

"I'm afraid of getting tangled up with you again! Falling for your charm, then being relegated to the back of the line." *Constantly telling myself I can change you if only I try harder.* "You have your life exactly as you shaped it. But I don't want to *fit* in with your life, Tate. I want to be part of—"

She bit the rest off before she said things she didn't mean.

Needing to create some semblance of distance between them, she locked her arms over her chest. "Read my lips. We're past tense, Tate."

The dimple in his cheek appeared as he chuckled. "Donna, that kiss was definitely present tense."

"I won't deny we still share a sexual chemistry…"

"Let's work from that point." He came closer.

Trembling inside and out, she stepped back. "It took time to get over you. I have my own life. I'm well respected." Hell, she respected herself and didn't intend for that to change.

"You work too hard." His curled knuckle stroked her cheek. "You need a break."

"You're right. I do need a break, Tate. From you and your manipulations. I'm taking a cab to the airport, with or without you."

The wide ledge of his shoulders went back, then he shrugged. "Fine."

She held her breath, waiting for more.

Sliding both hands into his trouser pockets, he tucked in his chin. "I'm not the type to force a lady, Donna, you know that."

As if he would ever need to use force. An encouraging touch here, an enticing stroke there… She wouldn't be the only woman to have liquefied beneath his skills in the bedroom.

Pushing aside the image of his bed—with them in it—she gathered her wits. The often seductive slant of his mouth appeared resigned. In fact, he looked at ease with her decision. As if…he were now as eager as she was to leave.

Her crossed arms fell to her sides and she sent

him a grudging smile. "Well, all I can say is I'm glad you're taking this so well."

"I don't continue to waste time on lost causes."

She flinched at the twinge beneath her ribs. Yes, she knew that from old. And that was exactly how she wanted it. Over and done with. For good.

Retracting his hands from his pockets, he started down the path—not the one they'd walked down earlier. This path was marked by a waist-high wooden sign that read, Private Poinsettia Accommodation.

"I'll grab my stuff," he tossed over one shoulder, "and we'll leave."

Next minute, she was alone. Music started up behind her, evening shadows crept in, and her poor brain seized up more. Grab his stuff… He meant go to his reserved bungalow where some of his belongings must already be stashed.

Like a cymbal clap, another thought struck. She narrowed her eyes and slowly grinned. Of course! This was a sham, a trick to leave her here, off balance, wondering, so she would eventually follow and end up smack-dab in his lair and he could—

Down the path, Tate reappeared from behind an evergreen spray of pigmy date palms. Black briefcase in hand, along with a bag she now recognized as a small overnighter, he was moving toward her quickly. Her throat constricted.

Heck...he really was eager to go.

Tate didn't so much join her as stride right past. While her foolish heart teetered then dropped to the ground, he stopped, turned and jerked his head at her. "You coming?"

She was about to mumble something half intelligent when he swore and strode back past again. "Left my phone on the table."

She blinked after him. Left alone again...with a night bird calling, poolside music playing and her self-conscious thoughts going wild. She'd never felt less attractive, not even as a gangly teenager with an embarrassing overbite.

How conceited to think the indomitable Tate Bridges would put up a fight for her. He'd thought he had a good chance, but clearly he wasn't overly concerned one way or the other. How ludicrous to believe he still cared enough.

Kicking herself, she shook her head. He had never cared for her the way she'd cared for him. Still cared, to be painfully honest.

Endless minutes ticked by. Finally she spied movement down the path, then glimpsed him, phone to ear, as he paced out from behind the pigmy palms, then back, out of sight once more.

Her sandaled foot grated up the sand then took one hesitant step forward. If he was stuck on some business call or had finally tracked down a troubled Blade, who knew how long the call would last.

Time rolled on. Her pulse started to pound and palms began to sweat. Counting the seconds, she laced her hands and squeezed.

Her heart leapt when she saw Tate pace into view. And out of sight again.

That does it.

She huffed and started off. This was absurd. She knew all about Tate and his phone calls. He'd shown up over an hour late at a restaurant once when he'd got "stuck." She would simply tell him she was leaving.

She glimpsed just a bit of him before he ducked into the private bungalow. Arriving at the door to the humble-looking hideaway, her step faltered. The thatched roof cottage gave the impression of complete isolation; the pool music was a distant percussive thump, the surrounding trees a picturesque natural screen. Tate's briefcase sat unattended on one of two rattan chairs on the open verandah.

Senses prickling, she listened to Tate's conversation traveling from inside—something to do with a news editor walking out. How much longer? Damn the man, had he completely forgotten about her? She would not be shoved aside again.

As she mounted the three stairs, the spa bath at the far end of the verandah caught her eye. Her center contracted as a wistful ribbon wound around her heart. An invisible string tugged her closer until she was bending, her hand drifting through the soft bubbling water.

Mango and lime underpinned by jasmine...

She knew the scent, would never forget it. It took her back to the best week of her life. To a time when she and Tate had been happy, with only themselves to worry about and no outside cares demanding his time. With all her heart she had believed in them.

Believed in their future.

Her concentration shifted and she frowned. It was quiet. No one-sided conversation filtering out. Tate had finished his call and, clearly, she was finished here.

She didn't hear but rather felt him behind her. Holding herself taut, she gradually turned.

His eyes roamed first her face then the full length of her still body. His eyebrows slowly pinched before his gaze eased up to pierce hers.

As he started toward her, each step measured and filled with unadorned purpose, her own legs lost strength. Halfway to her, he undid the first button on his shirt, then the next.

Her breathing shallowed out before falling to uneven snatches of air when, still walking, he pulled the shirttails from his pants.

Her voice came out a squeak. "Tate…I don't… this isn't…"

Every sip of oxygen left her lungs as he lifted her off the ground. She found herself slung in the steely hammock of his arms, his bare chest hot and inviting.

"Please…"

How to end that sentence? *Please don't?* If that were true, why did it seem her entire life was reduced to this moment?

After kicking off his loafers, he ascended the steps to the spa's wooden platform then down into the swirling frothing pool. As the water lapped her bottom, he focused on her lips and murmured in a deep level voice, "I won't kiss you."

The unbearable expectation at her center coiled higher, tighter. She swallowed against the nerves fluttering in her throat.

"You won't?"

His smile confirmed it. "You're going to kiss me."

She swallowed again. "I am?"

"And you'll keep on kissing—" his mouth dropped closer "—and kissing—" closer "—and then…"

Drowning in him, she threaded a weak arm around his neck and brought him down to her parted lips.

"Then—" Lord help her "—I'll kiss you again."

Five

The fact that they were fully clothed didn't matter. Donna clung to Tate's neck, her mouth fused to his, knowing soon everything would be shed—clothes, inhibitions, doubt.

As he brought her higher into his arms, deepening the kiss, she understood that at this moment history played no part in her desire for him. If aching for his embrace was wrong, so be it. If longing for the pleasure only his body gave was bad, she didn't care. She was so tired of being "strong" and "good."

She found great satisfaction in her profession,

but helping clients to cope with life's problems took its toll. Instead of easing others' pain, tonight she only wished to salve her own. And Tate's hard-muscled ministrations were just the balm.

Gradually his mouth released hers and she found herself being lowered to stand in the churning scented pool. As warm water massaged and tickled her thighs, she drank in the vision of Tate's solid bronzed chest. The shirt, which he'd finished unbuttoning, hung on his shoulders. Her fingers itched to remove it and savor the full intoxicating effects of his bared torso and arms.

As if reading her mind, he cocked one dark eyebrow. "Do it."

A tremor of guilty pleasure ripped through her veins. Heart racing, she exhaled slowly and slipped the fabric off his back. The shirt fell and swirled off through the suds. She couldn't keep her eyes from the captivating sight before her.

Tate's physique was even more masculine than she remembered…big biceps, strained and dangerous…perfectly honed pectorals pleading for her touch. His abdomen, defined by rungs of tanned muscle, naturally drew her attention down to a dark leather belt resting on his lean hips.

He said, "My turn."

Her breath burned in her lungs as he came

forward to kiss her temple at the same time his fingers delved behind her neck. Effortlessly he released the knot then, holding one corner, dragged the batik fabric from her body. Bending, he swept the sarong through the water, caught his shirt along the way and tossed both garments toward the vacant rattan chair.

While she stood before him—exposed, vulnerable, alive—he frowned playfully. "Nope. Still not even."

His large hands first circled her throat then traveled down the receptive curves where her neck met her collarbone. Shaky with anticipation, she let her eyes drift shut. She was a trembling, desperate, mindless mass, and he'd barely touched her.

"Donna, open your eyes."

A command? This minute he could say anything, do anything, and she would gladly obey.

Satisfied once she'd fixed her gaze on his, his line of vision scanned south, sizzling along her throat and across to where his left hand rested lightly on her swimsuit strap. Afraid her legs might dissolve beneath her, she watched the thick fringes of his lashes blink once before his hand slid meticulously down. One side of her swimsuit went, too.

His chest inflated as his lidded gaze soaked up the view. His fingers measured the lower arc of her breast, tested the weight then sculpted a stroke that ended with his thumb and forefinger gently pinching the tip. Overcome by exquisite weakness, she gripped his hips to stop from toppling forward.

With the same degree of skill, he drew the other strap down. Hands bracing her upper arms, he brought her closer, till his lowered mouth covered one aching nipple. His tongue worked around the peak, flicking, sucking, before, teeth skimming, he drew away.

Donna moaned. She was near frantic with longing to have him do it again.

When he released her arms, she slunk down, sighing as the water lapped her tummy, chest, throat. Acutely aware of Tate releasing his belt, unzipping his trousers, her anticipation wound ever higher until he finally let them fall.

Her throat swelled at the sight of him.

Pure male perfection.

After tossing out the last of his clothes, he lowered into the water and moved over to her. Kissing her, he maneuvered the rest of the swimsuit down over her hips and from her pliant legs. Her sandals slipped off along with the yellow Lycra. At last they were naked…natural and meant to be.

Growling his satisfaction, he twirled her over onto his lap. With his back propped against the spa wall, his mouth descended to sample her other breast. Lost in rapture, Donna arched back until her hair floated and trailed in the water behind her.

Conscious of the swell of his arousal resting between her legs, she sighed as he caressed her where her body needed it most. When his touch lightly circled, she shuddered against the almost violent push of pleasure. Afraid he might be side-tracked, she held his hand there and pulled herself back up toward him till her chest lay sloped against his. With her other hand she found him—hard as stone, hotter than a brand.

His throat hummed as he rubbed his bristled chin against her jaw. "You feel so good."

She nipped his lower lip in reply.

His magic had whisked her past the point of no return, and yet she knew this went against every-thing she'd vowed to avoid. The man had left her heart in tatters. Five years on he'd blatantly disre-garded her feelings and worth again.

Still, here she was...helpless in his arms. She wouldn't consider words like *careful,* or *conscience,* or *guilt.* Not a night passed where she didn't lay her head on the pillow and wish for the comfort of his physical heat.

Now she had him—Tate Bridges rippling with vitality, lulling her toward a precipice that tonight she would willingly fling herself from. Some time away from duty, sweet memories to hold on to and smile back on. Especially when he stroked there.

"We need protection."

His announcement jolted her back. They felt so close, it was torture to agree. She'd had no lovers since Tate, but other considerations shouldn't be ignored, no matter how desperately she wanted him.

He moved first. Standing thigh-deep in the bubbles, he took her hand and drew her up. He led her from the spa, dripping and deliciously warm, over the timber boards, through the bungalow entrance, then into the dusk-filled bedroom.

He shook out one of two large white towels, which lay on the gold brocade quilt, and patted her—hair, throat, shoulders, ribs. He gave every inch his full attention until she was dry all over. When he was satisfied, and she was biting her inside cheek against the urge to push him back onto the spread, he scrubbed his chest with the towel then dropped it at their feet. He moved to fling back the quilt then returned. With the barest of smiles, he circled her, edging her around till she was forced to sit then crawl backward over the sheets.

With her in position, he rummaged around his overnighter and retrieved one small square wrap. His husky voice carried in the looming darkness.

"Don't worry, I have more."

She flinched at the admission but smothered the hurt. Of course, he was prepared. And a part of her was flattered by his forethought. He still wanted her, after all these years. The glaring truth was she wanted him, too.

Foil wrap in hand, he prowled up over the embroidered silk. As if too much time had been wasted, he pinned her beneath him, hands above her head, and captured her mouth with his. Fireworks exploded throughout her hypersensitive body. Soon he would take her. The anticipation was blissful agony.

His hand sailed down the curve of her waist, over her hip and across to find her feverishly ready. After securing the condom, he eased inside her. She sighed and moved to meet him as his lips brushed her brow.

Within moments, the hypnotic grind and rhythm built to near self-combustion.

She found her breath and whispered against his ear, "Don't hold back."

Six

Hands cupping her head, Tate smiled at Donna's words. As he moved he murmured close to her lips, "Five years without you. This kind of pleasure is a crime."

His mouth dropped to cover her parted lips. When his tongue found hers, hot and hungry, the intensity leapt from high to clearing-the-stratosphere. Already he anticipated the next time, and the next.

The slim column of her neck arced. The lock of her thighs squeezed before her legs twined over his to help drive him in. Sweet heaven, he'd like this to last, but neither of them were superhuman.

Donna made that long, purring sound in her throat he'd once been so familiar with. She was close. His eyes closed as the urge to succumb challenged every switched-on cell in his body.

She whispered his name, then sucked her lips in and rolled her head first to one side then the next. He concentrated only on tangibles—position, sensation—and held her tighter.

It was time.

The release shot through his veins. Beneath him, Donna writhed and clung on as if the world had fallen away and he was her only anchor. The pulsing echoed in his head, compounded low in his belly.

Yes, paradise had never felt so good.

The peak lasted a lifetime...and not nearly long enough. As the throbbing eased his face lifted from her hair. Filling his lungs, he saw she was smiling, too, but her sparkling eyes already hinted at doubts.

Biting down against the jolt in his gut, he traced a path with his fingertip from her temple down her cheek. He kissed her nose.

"Welcome back."

But as her gaze held his, the smile slipped. Long lashes fluttered when she blinked several times. "I don't know what just happened."

He twined a lock of her fair hair around his finger. "I'd be happy to explain in greater detail."

Her frown verged on playful. "Sex was always good between us. That was never the issue."

He kissed the curve of her shoulder. "It's one hell of an issue now."

Her voice was almost firm. "This can't happen again, Tate. For so many reasons. If anyone finds out we're romantically involved while I'm assigned to your brother's case…" Shuddering, she wriggled out from under him. "I couldn't face my peers, or myself, again."

When she tried to leave his bed, he tugged her back, his arm locking her in place beside him. He gave her a squeeze. "No one will find out."

"That's not the point. What we've done crosses the line." Her fist clenched low on her stomach. "I should never have let you push me into seeing Blade in the first place."

Tate frowned. His blackmail threat had been empty. That story about her would never air, but now more than ever he couldn't let her know. She would remove herself from the case and there was always the chance his brother might be stuck with a negative report from another psychologist. Equally disturbing—he would lose whatever personal hold he had on Donna.

Getting her back in his bed hadn't been his initial objective, no matter what she might believe. Although it still needled that she'd cut him off after their engagement party without so much as a decent conversation, he'd come to accept—even welcome in a way—that they would never be husband and wife.

Clearly he wasn't made for marriage and the lifetime of obligations that followed. He had more than enough responsibility already. But renewing their lovers relationship? That was a different story.

Sure, he had regrets, but enjoying Donna's body again, feeling how she wanted him, too, wasn't one of them. She must realize he would never go ahead and crucify her with a report that would destroy her reputation.

This week, his private investigator had confirmed she'd had no lover since him. He might have tempted her with stolen kisses, but she'd willingly surrendered to the bait. Actions spoke louder than words.

She wanted to be here—naked, together—as much as he.

He moved onto his side and gathered her closer. Her silken curves fired up his blood once more. He didn't want to talk, unless it was about making love.

"Let's keep the world outside for now." He gently cradled her head and circled her temple with his thumb. "We have three days together. And I want them just to be about us."

Before he could seal that declaration with a kiss,

she pushed against him and eased out of bed. He regretted losing her warmth, but the view of her naked body made up for it.

Her full breasts rose and fell with each uneven breath. In the muted light filtering through a break in the bedroom curtains, her cheeks looked flushed—from residual pleasure or fresh angst?

"You're not listening, Tate. I *can't* get involved, and not only for professional reasons. You haven't changed. If anything, you're more stubborn than ever."

Her back slowly straightened. "I'm going to catch that flight." She found a towel and wrapped it around herself.

Adrenaline spiked through his system. But he controlled the rev and sat up slowly, deliberately. "You'll stay with me."

"I might have just done the dumbest thing in my life, but I'm not completely stupid."

He felt a muscle tick in his cheek. "We had problems in the past but tonight we can take the first step in moving forward."

"Nice try, but you're a stone, and stone doesn't change."

"Have you seen the Grand Canyon?"

"We don't have ten million years."

Irritation prickled the back of his neck. "You

really ought to cut yourself some slack. Carrying all that guilt around must be tiring."

She stopped fiddling with her slipping towel and simply glared at him. "Besides accommodating you today, what do I have to feel guilty about?"

Tate groaned. Both he and Donna had taken on heavy personal loads; at times he felt the weight so intensely he thought his back might break. In that way they were very similar but for one vital difference.

No matter how hard he tried to make up for his part in his parents' deaths, he would never feel fully redeemed. But at least he acknowledged that torment for what it was—personal blame.

His haunted sense of loyalty had contributed to their relationship's breakdown, but so had hers. When he'd known her last, he'd held his tongue when perhaps he should have pressed her.

He lowered his voice. "We both know why you're desperate to get these extra safe houses off the ground."

Her gaze held before darting to the left. "There's a shortage of accommodation, which means fewer options for women in trouble who need a place to stay."

A well-rehearsed response.

"And?"

Her mouth opened and closed before she manufactured a casual tone. "A friend…a close friend was also an inspiration."

"You and Judith lived together in your last foster home."

Abandoned as a baby, Donna had become a ward of the state. She'd spoken to him about it only once. Given the tight line of her mouth now, she'd still rather not discuss it. She'd appreciate his next point even less.

"The year we were together," he continued, "Judith died, a victim of domestic homicide." He hesitated, but pushed on. "You couldn't save her, Donna."

She closed her eyes and winced. "I told her to move into my apartment, but she said she didn't want to put me in any kind of danger."

"But there *was* a shelter she could have gone to?"

She frowned, irritated. "You know all this."

He was certain he *didn't* know it all. More to the point, he suspected Donna needed to face it now before they could move on.

She looked at him hard before shifting her weight and pushing out the words.

"Judith's father had also been abusive. Before being placed in foster care, she spent a lot of time with her mother in shelters. She had horrible memories of living with groups of strangers whenever her home life erupted. So she wanted to wait for an individual house or duplex where she could have some privacy. But whenever one eventually freed up, she'd talk herself out of leaving."

Not looking at Tate, but rather through him, Donna held her towel tight at her breast. "Judith hadn't gone to college. She didn't have any job at that stage, and she refused to take money from me." Her eyes blazed and watered then she growled, "How I wish she'd never met that man."

Seemed he'd turned on a tap. Those last months they'd been together, she'd refused to talk about Judith's death. She'd grown more and more sullen because, as far as he could fathom, she couldn't save her friend and therefore deserved to be punished. Like a self-fulfilling prophesy, eight weeks after the funeral, he and Donna were no longer a couple.

She pushed some drying hair behind her ear. "Rehashing this is pointless."

He raised his brows. She was the one doing the talking. And the message was loud and clear: Donna Wilks helped people. Donna couldn't help her friend. Therefore, Donna didn't deserve happiness.

She'd brought down the final ax on their relationship and in hindsight perhaps that had been best. Each had their responsibilities, and ghosts, to serve. But now that the dust had settled, one force linked them still: he wanted her and she wanted him. Weddings were no longer the issue. But they could comfort each other, every night if they wished, and wasn't that a good thing?

He smiled softly and patted the sheet. "You're tired. Forget about planes. Come back here and relax."

Let me hold you and you can hold me.

"Relax? That's real cute coming from an extortionist."

He frowned at her jaded look.

Enough talk.

He reached over and caught her waist. As she looked at him with anger, mistrust and desire in her eyes, he wanted to say, *I won't let anything hurt you.* But, given her last comment and his current inability to refute it, he bit those words off. Two others came to mind. His throat ached as he said them.

"Come back."

Her mouth trembled before an impassive look hardened her face and her frame tensed. "I have enough to regret. All I want is to stand under a long hot shower, get dressed and go."

After a drawn-out moment, he nodded. Tomorrow morning he'd be in there with her, sponging her back. She might have won this battle, but he would win the war.

As she moved into the attached bathroom, the

bedside extension caught his eye. The message light was blinking red. His mind flew in a circle. Blade or anyone at the station would use his cell number.

He stabbed the message button and listened. As the shower water began to hiss, Tate sank down onto the mattress. Given who had left that message for Donna, and the tone of that voice, guess their secret was out.

Seven

Donna left the bathroom in an oversized guest robe, fluffing one side of her shampooed hair with a fresh towel. She stopped in her tracks at the sight greeting her.

Tate was pouring champagne. And he hadn't dressed.

Her already warm skin began to sizzle as her respiratory picked up pace. He was playing a scintillating game of seduction and this was full-throttle, second-half kickoff.

Drawn but also determined, she dropped the

towel inside the bathroom and knotted her arms over her chest. "*That's* a waste of time."

She'd made one doozy of a slip, but all was not lost. No one need know she'd fallen into bed with her blackmailer, her ex-lover. Now she merely had to keep her head and make it out of here intact.

Tate peered over his big bare shoulder as if he'd forgotten she'd been in the next room. "I've only poured one glass." He took a sip. "Not French but still very fine."

As he turned to stopper the bottle, she glared. He knew she loved champagne, but she was in no mood for celebrating. For all intents and purposes, he'd cross-examined her, and only minutes after making love. He was merciless. Worse, she would never admit it, but he had made a valid and insightful point.

She felt responsible for Judith's death, even though she knew she shouldn't. As a friend or therapist she could listen and make suggestions for change, but she couldn't make problems disappear, or force others to make smart choices. It was frustrating, painful, but true. No human being could make another end a self-destructive relationship.

Tate lifted a chrome lid to reveal a colorful fruit and cheese platter, causing her taste buds to tingle. But her mouth watered more at the sight of Tate's toned back, the way his muscles rippled across the polished flesh. His presence dominated the room, despite wearing nothing but a towel lashed around his lean hips.

As he turned, her midsection contracted at his crooked smile. No one had a right to look that gorgeous.

"This is an appetizer," he said. "Room service is twenty-four hours so we don't need to think about dinner yet."

Garnering every molecule of strength, she waved her hands. "I'll eat something on the plane."

Declining to comment, he strolled over with a cracker and cheese. He bit off half. Before she could object, he slipped the other half past her lips. Grunting, she pushed his hand away.

His eyes crinkled. "It's not blue vein. Don't worry."

She wasn't worried about mold. She worried about itching to touch his hard, smooth body now and paying with her heart later.

As he crossed back to the platter, she slowly chewed and remembered how as teens living with the same foster family, she and Judith had studied through the day and giggled through the night, dreaming about the more sophisticated breed of bad boy—irresistible enigmas with jet-black hair, piercing blue eyes and untamable hearts. After her friend's funeral, those memories had clawed at

Donna's gut and eaten at her brain until she'd come to her senses and ended a relationship that could only continue to bring her pain.

She hadn't been able to save her friend but she had saved herself. Not from physical harm—Tate would *never* physically hurt her—but rather from emotional grief. Her series of safe houses would help others in Judith's situation restore their confidence, their identities, maybe even save their lives.

She tightened the tie of her robe.

Nothing and no one would keep her from fulfilling that goal, the promise she'd made to herself.

Tate cut the fruit. "I had your belongings sent for."

Donna frowned.

He edged over a seductive look. "Did you really expect me to keep you here tied up and naked?"

Her tummy fluttered. She shoved that evocative thought aside and replaced it with another, more sensible one. Having her clothes sent over simply saved her organizing it herself. If she were in a more generous mood, she might thank him.

He waved a slice of mango. "Want some?"

As she shook her head, his mouth closed over the fruit. She could taste the sweetness and licked her lips. She remembered the last time they'd been at this resort, how she'd rubbed mango-scented oil on his chest and he'd rubbed her—

With a start, she pulled herself back from the past. A little light-headed, she spied her bag and walked toward the bed.

In a hurry, she tore her wrinkle-proof dress from the tote bag. A piece of jewelry came with it and fell on the rug at her feet. Her heart sprang to her throat.

She swooped down to grab it, but Tate, there in a blink, beat her to it.

He dangled the gold links before her. "Well, well…I wondered if you'd kept this."

Snatching the watch from his fingers, she down-played the significance of his discovery. "It's an expensive and beautiful watch. Why wouldn't I still have it?"

His sizzling gaze moved over her lips down to her neck, heating her skin. His smile grew broader.

"You weren't wearing it this morning. I'd have noticed." He lightly touched her left wrist.

Although her flesh responded, she refused the blatant come-on and turned away. Begging her heart to quit thumping, she shucked back one shoulder with a haughty air. "I couldn't find my other watch and grabbed this in a hurry on the way out. I forgot to put it on."

That was her story and she'd stick to it. She wouldn't admit that after seeing him again, she'd had a crushing desire to drag the watch from the bottom of her jewelry box to wear for the first time in years.

Feeling Tate behind her—his mesmerizing heat—she held herself tight. Her breath caught in her chest as his gravelly voice rumbled and tickled her ear.

"Nice try," he teased, "but you're a lousy liar."

"Yet others do it so well." She gave him a pointed glare.

The phone buzzed. Rather than answer it, Tate sauntered back to the platter and champagne bucket.

He raised a second chilled glass, tracing a finger down its running condensation. "Sure you won't have one? It's your favorite."

All the more reason to decline. Champagne slid down easier than water but the bubbles went straight to her head. She needed her wits about her, these next few moments more than ever.

The phone kept ringing.

She glanced between the extension and Tate. On her way to the bathroom to change, her dress and underwear in hand, she jerked her chin. "Are you going to get that?"

Shoulders holding up the wall, he crossed one ankle over the other and raised his glass. "I'm off duty."

A thread of disquiet wove through her. Tate was never off duty.

Her pace eased up. "Did I hear it ring while I was in the shower?"

"Nope." He tipped the glass to his mouth, ready to sip. "Probably just housekeeping."

A chill scuttled up her spine. Tate couldn't resist answering a call, no matter the time of day, no matter where they were. When they'd dated, it had driven her nuts. The only time he refused to pick up was if they were making love. Something was wrong and from his overly nonchalant mood, she couldn't help but believe she was involved.

She did a one-eighty and headed for the phone. Setting down his glass, Tate moved, too. Their darting hands collided on the receiver, hers beating his by a nanosecond. Yanking the handset away, she jammed it to her ear.

"Who is this?"

"Donna?" A female voice croaked down the line. "Hallelujah! Do you realize I've tried to contact you all day?"

A ghastly sinking feeling dropped from the back of her throat to her heels.

"Donna, *Donna?* Are you there?"

She pried her tongue from the roof of her mouth to wring out two words. "Mrs. deWalters." She noticed Tate heading toward the champagne and her shock at hearing the other woman's voice segued into red-tinged rage. "Did you try this number earlier?"

"I left a message. Your cell is off, or out of range, or perhaps it's broken. I insisted your assistant divulge your whereabouts. Reception put me through to your room."

Though Tate purposely ignored her, she slid him a poisonous glare. So much for anonymity.

A sudden thought struck her. Did Mrs. deWalters have any idea who shared her reservation?

The older woman huffed on the other end of the line. "Clearly you've forgotten our appointment tomorrow?"

Donna's more immediate dilemma clicked back into sharp focus. Her mind flicked through a mental calendar. "We have an appointment Wednesday, Mrs. deWalters, not tomorrow."

"I told you last Saturday evening to call me Maeve. And we'd agreed on tomorrow, not Wednesday, to meet."

Donna stuttered as her brain froze and face burned. Maeve deWalters was wrong, but the grande dame also carried some important clout. Donna needed her ongoing financial support. Her pride had no place in this relationship. She would agree with everything, do anything, Maeve deWalters said.

Donna held the phone tighter. "Tomorrow… where and when?"

"Hardly matters now." She sniffed. "You're on vacation."

Oh God, she had to salvage this situation and quickly. "No, no. Not vacation. This is strictly business and I'm coming back tonight."

"Then why the reservation, pet? I mean, it's really none of my business…"

Donna enunciated each word. "I will be back by morning, Mrs. deWalters—"

"Maeve. I told you to call me Maeve." Her voice was frosty now. "Are you paying attention? You seem distracted."

Donna barely held off from screaming, first over the line, then at Tate. If he hadn't twisted her arm into coming here…if she hadn't been so gullible…

Curling her toes, she gritted her teeth and silently counted to three.

"I'll be there, Maeve. Perhaps we could have breakfast together somewhere nice then visit the properties—"

"The very reason for my call. I can't make it now until Wednesday. But you'd sounded so eager, I wanted to give you a hearing before I speak with my fund-raising committee first thing Monday. Yet I fear now I've caught you at an inopportune time."

Not an apology. More a dig.

Their misunderstanding needed repairing, but this conversation was only adding to the confusion. Besides, she was shaking too much to concentrate on anything other than the possibility of everything she'd worked for falling apart.

Maeve might discover she was here with her old enemy. The Registration Board might find out too, or the magistrate on Blade's case. This time last week her life had been sailing a crest. Tonight it was close to smashing on the rocks.

She tried to think calmly and control the quaver in her voice. "I'm about to leave to catch a plane, so, yes, perhaps it would be best to leave this conversation until Wednesday." As originally planned, she wanted to add.

A put-upon sigh followed. "Do put it in your calendar, pet."

Donna held off slamming the phone and walked straight to her handbag. Her cell phone's volume had been bumped down, probably pushed against something, and there was a stack of messages, several from Maeve as well as April, no doubt warning her.

Her hand shook. She wanted to hurl the cell at the wall, but it wasn't the phone's fault. Hell, it wasn't even Tate's. It was hers for being pathetically weak, buckling beneath his demands and coming here in the first place. A brief return to Eden was so not worth it.

Face burning, she whirled on him. "You listened to her message, didn't you?" Donna didn't wait for an answer. "Is there even a tiny part of you that cares about what you've done?"

He had sabotaged her position, jeopardized her goal, all to meet his own objectives. How typical. How very, very Tate.

His strong jaw kicked up. "Maeve deWalters is a crony who attained her position through marriage and her fortune through corruption. Believe me, you'd do better to look elsewhere for support."

Like from him? How laughable.

She marched for the bathroom. "You have no evidence of corruption or she'd be the first to know."

"And the public would be second."

At the bathroom doorway, she snapped around. "Because of media or family-feud justice?"

"A whole bunch of both."

With a purposeful gleam in his eye, he stalked toward her.

Swallowing hard, she turned away from him. "I'm getting out of here now before you really screw things up."

His arm shot out, caught hers and drew her close. As her clothes fell to the floor, he urged her against his chest. She didn't want him handling her, couldn't he see? Her body might betray her, trying its best to respond to his power, but surely he could read the expression on her face. Damn it, she was serious!

She struggled. "Let me *go*."

"You don't have to pretend," he told her. "This isn't Sydney, there are no public eyes upon us. We're completely isolated. You can hide from everything here—including yourself—if you want."

He urged her closer. She felt the hardness of his erection against her belly, and she smothered a moan before it left her throat.

His hand pressed a hypnotic circle at the base of her spine. "Be honest...when was the last time you felt so good?"

The answer was too easy: the last time they were here together. But things were different now. *He* might not have changed but she had.

How dare he play with her life? He might dislike the deWalters family, but his opinion mattered little where her life's work was concerned.

Determined not to let that fact fade beneath a haze of passion, she ignored the heartbeat pulsing a time-old message in her womb and settled her mind firmly on escape. "When is the next flight out?"

Grinning, he challenged her with his eyes. "We've missed it."

She didn't believe him. Still, this wasn't a major city with a revolving door of commuter fights. She needed an alternative.

"A private plane then."

His eyes flashed and too late she realized what she'd said. Automatically her heart went out to him. He avoided conversations about small aircraft. Too many bad memories. Knowing the story, she understood.

"There's the phone." He nodded his head to the bedside table. "I won't stop you." Yet his hands on her hips held her firm.

"A bus," she managed in a throaty voice.

"I'll beat you back to Sydney—" he nipped her ear "—and have had a relaxing couple of days to boot."

"Staying with you won't make a difference," she ground out. "No matter how much you push, I won't let you intimidate me."

"Is that right?" He sucked her lobe and her body glowed red-hot.

"I will give Blade a fair assessment," she said, stifling a moan, "nothing more, nothing less."

"Donna, shh. This isn't about work. What we're doing now is all about pleasure."

This situation had deteriorated so quickly. Why had she thought it would be any different? Tate was the one man who could evoke this delirious abandon in her. From the moment they'd met, she had wanted no one else.

If he looked at her with those hot eyes, reached for her with that hot touch, the fight was lost. That's why she'd refused to see him after their engagement party. He didn't need to know about that one weak moment a few weeks later when she'd gone to see him and had inadvertently witnessed just how little he'd missed her.

He ground against her, combing his hands through her hair. Cupping her head, he kissed her thoroughly. By the time she came up for air, her lips were on fire and her mind was mush. How she managed a threat of her own was nothing short of a miracle.

"Maybe I should go to the judge and tell him about your ultimatum."

The grip on her head tightened. "Not a good idea. You should avoid throwing suspicion upon yourself."

"And a weekend away together doesn't look suspicious?"

He released her to peel the robe from her shoulders so only the tie on her hips kept it from falling. As his chest grazed her tender nipples, she bit her lip.

His teeth skimmed her neck. "Your reputation will remain intact. No one will find out."

"Except the biggest gossip in Sydney."

He growled. "Maeve deWalters knows nothing."

Well, not yet.

She was walking a tightrope that could snap at any moment. Secrets had a habit of revealing themselves when least expected.

Hands skimming her sides, he lowered himself to one knee, gifting a kiss on each of her breasts, her rib cage, the square inch above her navel. She closed her eyes at the sensations. His method and skill were infinitely fine. Like champagne bubbles, he made her head spin.

Three days, he'd said. How could it hurt?

Her resolve gone, she sighed and held his head. "You won't leak anything to anyone. Promise?"

A hum in his throat, he parted the robe and drew a bone-melting line with his tongue between her legs.

"I promise."

Eight

If someone won't admit they have a problem, they're likely to continue making the same mistakes.

Late Sunday morning, Donna remembered that advice, wishing it didn't so aptly apply to herself. The irony was the more time she spent with Tate the more she could admit to the problem, and the less she wanted to do anything about it.

Lying sloped across a beach blanket, head in hand, she watched him dive through the rough foam-laced waves. The sun was warm on her skin. A picnic basket lay crooked in the sand beside her.

She would have a glass of champagne with lunch

and make love with Tate again after that—relive the incomparable thrill of joining with the only man on earth who could make her forget to breathe.

No one would understand. Hell, she didn't understand or forgive herself. She would still give Blade the assessment she believed he deserved—nothing would sway her there, not even Tate's diminishing threat of having that story aired. But if people uncovered this liaison, she wouldn't blame them for thinking all was not aboveboard.

Squeezing her eyes shut, she cursed under her breath.

These feelings for Tate were not only overwhelming, they were all-consuming. She knew she should be stronger, hated herself for being so damn weak. Only people who had experienced this same giddy sense of euphoria could possibly understand.

She didn't seem to have a choice, not here, where the past whispered at her ear and Tate was so alive and strong and real.

Tate jogged out from the ocean, kicking up water, smoothing hands back over wet hair, unconsciously exhibiting his incredible biceps. He looked unconquerable. Her lover. And she was—

Her heart rolled over.

His mistress?

He fell on his knees and, palms on thighs, shook

out his hair. Despite her mood, she laughed as water sprayed in an arc.

Sitting up, she wiped her arms. "Hey, watch it!"

His lopsided grin grew. "Or you'll do what?"

Or I'll burn tomorrow's flight reservations and beg you to keep me here.

She let out a breath and managed a smile. "You don't want to know."

"Bet I do." Eyes smoldering, he prowled toward her on all fours.

A nervous laugh bubbled up inside her. Yesterday he'd surprised her by buying her a bikini from the resort boutique. It was far more revealing than one she might have chosen herself. Now his finger hooked into the gold ring linking the top's black triangles and tugged. "How are you placed for skinny-dipping?"

He angled his mouth over hers—cold and fresh covering warm and willing. Moving closer, his back and head curled over her. When their lips softly parted, she was dizzy and his chest was heaving.

That finger, hooked through the gold ring, rocked her right then left as his hungry gaze devoured her. "I can't decide if I like this better on or off."

A glimpse of decorum struggled through the delicious thick fog of her brain and her hand stopped his. "We're in the open."

He looked around and shrugged. "No people here. Be adventurous."

That yanked her right down from the clouds. She'd been adventurous—reckless—enough. They weren't eighteen, with few cares or responsibilities. In fact, they each had enormous responsibilities and they were ignoring them all. But tomorrow—and the consequences—would come soon enough.

Nerves gripping her stomach, she swiveled toward the basket. "Maybe we should eat back at the bungalow." Suddenly she felt very exposed.

"I'm all for retiring indoors." His hand skimmed across the shoulder he'd covered with oil just thirty minutes before. "But the label on the suntan lotion said we're safe outdoors for a couple more hours." As his hand circled, then slid down her arm, a spellbinding sensation fizzed along her veins. His deep rich voice rolled over her. "It's up to you."

Both options were dangerous.

If they stayed out here amidst the swaying palm fronds and fresh salty air, she could see them getting carried away. If they went back to the hideaway, her bikini wouldn't last much past the front door. Instantly she would be washed away on a slipstream of rising pleasure. But the moment her parachute landed and her feet touched the ground, her mind would begin to work again—what they were doing, the trust she was breaking—and then she'd just want to die.

Nothing was worth the guilt, not even this glorious time in the sun.

Tate moved to sit beside her and swept the champagne bottle from the basket. "Can I tempt you?"

Her attention drifted up from his footprint left in the sand to his transfixing blue eyes. She blinked, then frowned.

"No."

He chuckled and made himself more comfortable. "Too early?"

"Better than being too late."

He purposefully set the bottle back on the checked cloth before looking at her. "I feel a discussion coming on."

Her heartbeat skipped but, after forty hours laced with scintillating sex, it was time to talk instead of touch.

His regard was casual yet steely. "Don't kid yourself this is like the first time. This doesn't have to end badly. What we've enjoyed here has been good for us both."

"What we've enjoyed here is *wrong*." Feeling ill, she dropped her head into her hands. "The board is already investigating one allegation against me. And then there's Maeve, who is more than a little unhappy with me. I can't afford any more slipups. If Maeve discovers I'm involved with the Bridges family…if she finds out I'm romantically involved with you—"

Did she need to finish the sentence? If Maeve found out, the ball of disaster would begin to roll downhill. She'd lose her funding, she'd lose her reputation, but worse, on a personal level, she'd lose her self-respect by being publicly caught in Tate's web again. Come to think of it, she didn't have too much self-respect left at this point anyway.

Tate's jaw shifted as he reached into the picnic basket and retrieved a wrapped sandwich. "I told you, Maeve deWalters is on her way out."

A set of tiny warning antennae quivered. That wasn't the first time he'd implied Maeve was crooked. Could there be more than malice behind it? Maybe she should take a breath and actually listen. Or, better yet, ask some questions.

"You're saying she's corrupt?"

He chewed and nodded. "Undoubtedly."

Her tone was dry. "Don't be shocked, but people might think you're corrupt trying to lever a court judgment."

"I'm not shocked." He swallowed. "I don't care."

Her teeth clamped down. "Why, pray tell, why is it all right for you to try and bend the rules and not Maeve?"

Not that she agreed anyone should be above the law, herself included.

"Your question concerns the difference between a woman skimming the cream off charity coffers to feather her own bank account and a brother doing what he can to protect his own against an unjust prison term."

"You maintain that Blade's innocent." While not a lawyer, she knew of several defenses against assault, one of them self-defense. But Tate was side-stepping her issue. "Why does that give you the right to manipulate me?"

He skimmed a hand through his hair and considered her for a long tense moment. "Would it help if I said I was sorry?"

She nodded. "An apology might help...if I thought you meant it. But at this point, I'm afraid I need a whole lot more from you than that."

He was still for a long agonizing moment, before he peered up at the sun through squinted eyes then nodded. "What do you want to know?"

"I want to know why you're so protective of Libby and Blade. And tell me everything this time—not the superficial lines you used to feed me."

His parents had died; he'd become his siblings' guardian. She'd always understood and appreciated the sense of responsibility associated with that. But instinct said there had to be more to Tate's obsession with keeping his brother and sister protected.

"You know my parents died in a private plane crash. I wasn't long out of college," he continued. "I wanted to start living my life. Do what I wanted to do, when I wanted to do it. It happened around this time of year—close to Christmas. I had friends to visit, but my parents called wanting me to come home for a couple of days. They had an important dinner to attend in the Blue Mountains, and Blade—" He cleared his throat. "He was going through a rough patch."

She pressed her lips together. Although her training said "listen," it was difficult to keep her emotional distance where Tate was concerned.

He concentrated on the sand. "I argued. Told them to get a sitter, if they really needed it for a nineteen-year-old. I didn't see why Blade couldn't look after Libby. Why call me?"

He blew out a breath. "I turned up late, groaning and dragging my feet. They wanted me there at three. I arrived closer to six-thirty. At that stage my mother wasn't looking forward to a three-hour drive that included winding mountain roads, and arriving past fashionably late. My father often chartered private aircraft. They thought a light plane would get them there in half the time with half the hassle." His mouth swung to one side. "You know the rest."

His parents hadn't been able to take their car. Instead they'd hired a private aircraft. For reasons never explained, the plane had crashed twenty minutes from its destination. And Tate had been left with a guilt he could never assuage. The mist began to clear.

A hopping seagull flapped and leapt high as Tate tossed his sandwich. "And you want to hear the kicker?"

"Go on."

"The party they needed so desperately to attend was at the home of none other than Maeve deWalters."

Donna coughed. Oh, dear Lord. "They were friends?" She'd assumed the families had always been at odds.

"Never friends. Business acquaintances. Maeve's third husband spent a great deal of money on advertising with my father's still-fledgling network." A muscle in his bristled cheek jumped. "The party had been cancelled. Dear Maeve hadn't bothered to inform her less important guests."

Little wonder Tate tortured himself and carried around a metaphorical knife for Maeve as well. He believed through his self-centered acts he'd deprived his siblings, and himself, of their parents.

Searching Tate's eyes, she wrapped her arms around his strong neck and pulled herself near. She murmured against his ear, "You need to let it go."

She wanted to say he shouldn't blame himself, but she knew self-absolution didn't come easily. Nothing, not even time, fully washed away the stain.

He took her shoulders and gently pried her away. His jaw had never looked stronger, shadowed with two days' growth of beard. His dusky pink lips had never looked sexier, slanted and resigned.

"I'm fine with where I am, Donna. I know what I want. What I need to do." He pushed to his feet, his smile convincing, invincible. "Right now, I need to go battle more waves."

When they made love that afternoon, it was just as soul-lifting, but, amidst the tangle of sheets, their joining also seemed changed, somehow deeper and more sensitive…as if a layer had peeled away and what lay beneath was still too raw to look at, too dangerous to speak of.

Landing in Sydney the next day, Tate was his usual charming self. After mentioning he would be in touch regarding the assessment Blade needed, she reaffirmed that should she provide one, it would be completely honest. She couldn't decide whether he looked amused or all the more determined.

When the taxi dropped her off and they kissed goodbye, she tried to convince herself it would be their last. The choice hurt unbearably, but surely it was wiser to be strong, end this relationship and avoid the train wreck that awaited them around their next clandestine bend. The weekend had been remarkable, but over time his demanding character would increasingly tear at her soul.

The facts remained: he wanted her continued affections and she needed to regain her self-respect.

She didn't return his calls. She needed time to set her mind straight. Yet by Thursday morning her inner struggle had only gotten worse. The urge to buckle and see him again was overwhelming.

Weeks after their engagement-party fiasco, she'd been gripped by a similar urge to surrender. To this day Tate didn't know that she'd seen him embrace and kiss another woman. Now more than ever she should remember not only how deeply he'd hurt her by consistently putting her feelings last, but also how easily she'd been replaced.

As she sipped coffee at her kitchen counter, she flicked through the morning newspaper. When a feature article caught her eye, she focused and scanned the lines. Her fingers gradually slipped and coffee streamed to darken the page. As her blood pressure exploded, one image crystallized in her mind.

Tate on his knees making love to her, murmuring, *I promise.* And lying through his teeth.

Nine

"I can't believe you went through with it."

Tate took in Donna's scathing words, studied the scowl on her face and, for the first time in years, didn't quite know what to do.

A maddening pulse beat in his neck. He loosened his tie and, without invitation, slid into the café's red-vinyl booth beside her. The close proximity had immediate impact. Her fresh-flower scent, the flow of silken fair hair, the—

At a flash of irritation, he flipped a hand. "Take off those dark glasses—" he needed to see her eyes "—and we'll talk about this rationally."

"Rational for you or for me?" The frames hit the table with a *snap*. "There's a mountain of difference."

She reached blindly beside her and threw the morning paper on the grey laminate next to some faded fake roses and an empty coffee cup. A headline was circled in angry red:

Couch Therapy—Be Careful Who You Trust.

Tears edged her eyes, but her mouth remained firm. "I tell you any assessment will be completely honest then I don't return your calls. So you decide to give me a taste of what's in store if I refuse to give you precisely what you want." She winced. "Do you know what hurt the most? You didn't have the decency to warn me."

"Because I had nothing to do with it."

He dashed the paper, and his need to hold her, aside. Three days without her body next to his had felt like an eon. How had he survived so long before?

She smirked, but he glimpsed vulnerability beneath the hard shell. "So it's a huge coincidence that you blackmail me, throw in a little seduction, and when I still won't come to heel, a sneak preview of your threat happens to show up in the broadsheets."

Logic. "Am I the only one who had access to information regarding the complaint against you?"

Her long lashes blinked. "No."

"Does the article mention you by name?"

A question mark formed in the shadows of those turquoise eyes before her beautiful mouth hardened again. "Doesn't mean you're not behind it."

"It also doesn't confirm that I am. In fact, if I were the instigator, I'd more likely leak the info just before my show's debut. With your story as lead, the ratings would soar through the roof."

Her eyes narrowed at his dry look before she pushed up the sleeves of her white blouse. Her lace bra was a tantalizing shadow beneath the silk. Despite her hostility and this less-than-conducive situation, his blood began to race.

"Maybe you leaked this now to leave me guessing," she concluded, sounding uncertain. "Too unsettled to rock your boat."

His eye line dropped to the slender waistband of her tailored red skirt. He'd bet she hadn't eaten before or after she'd phoned him in a rage. Coffee wasn't enough. A good breakfast would help settle her down. She liked flapjacks with syrup. He'd order two stacks.

Glancing around the mostly deserted suburban café, he tried to catch the attention of a waiter busy lining up soda bottles in the front fridge.

Her harsh whisper was a warning at his ear. "Are you listening to me?"

Turning back, he refrained from dropping his

mouth over hers to silence her. Kissing was what she needed. In fact, they both needed to get back to what they did so well, rather than arguing over an incident that couldn't be undone. If he could fix it, damn it, he would.

"I'll say it once more. I did not leak that story."

But in a way he was grateful to whoever had. Donna hadn't returned his calls since their return from Queensland. And this meeting had more easily opened up a way for him to get to her. They were good together; she knew that as well as he. Whatever had come before, they'd work through it—he'd make certain.

Her expression jaded, she fell back against the vinyl. "Yeah, you're just so principled. Guess I have nothing to fear by saying this then." She tipped closer to look him squarely in the eye. "Your lawyer needs to find another patsy. I'm off Blade's case. You can do what you want about it—badger, growl, charm, if you like. Tactics won't make a scrap of difference. I'm sick of bouncing on your string. As of this second, I'm getting on with my life."

His head cocked.

Hell, she thought she meant it.

But the past few days couldn't be erased. They were bound now, differently than before, and for more reasons than one. He angled around so his bent trouser leg rested on the seat and she couldn't misread or avoid the conviction in his expression.

"Blade needs you."

I need you.

"I told you from the start, Blade has to face the consequences of his actions." Her expression changed. "So do I. You say he's innocent. I know I am. The best we can do is sit back, keep our noses clean, and trust in the system."

Trust in the system? He thrust back his shoulders. "I can't do that."

"You're going to have to," she said simply.

He refrained from mentioning he wasn't sure if Blade's prior offense was admissible. Donna wouldn't sympathize. She still didn't know what had lain at the heart of the trouble the night of their disastrous engagement party. At this juncture, she'd be less inclined than ever to believe it.

"Don't you want to know where my brother got to last Friday?" That night Blade had left a message to say he was okay and not to worry. But Donna didn't know anything beyond that. "He met up with Kristin and they're trying to sort out their problems."

He hoped the subtext wasn't too subtle.

She shook her head a little too fast. "That's none of my business anymore."

His chest tightened as a frisson of annoyance

speared right the way through. "Like Libby wasn't your business anymore five years ago?"

Her eyes flashed. "She was seventeen when we broke up. I couldn't see her again—" Her voice caught before she began again in a calmer tone. "I couldn't see her again without seeing you. You know how much I cared for Libby. She was like my sister."

But not in the truest sense of the word. Donna had grown up in foster care. From what he knew of her experience, with the possible exception of Judith, she'd never had any real family. Donna didn't quite understand—and he was loath to point it out—that despite her fondness, she *could* walk away from Libby; he could not.

His focus wandered to her finely boned fist resting on the newsprint. That ugly, practical, black leather band was wound around her wrist.

He took her hand. "Where's my watch?"

Her dawning smile was almost sad. "It's so important to you, isn't it? Seeing your cuff around my wrist. Thinking you own me."

She was right, of course. He *did* want that sense of ownership. And he wanted *her* so much—but not too close.

The secret of success was delegation. He could do that with work, but personal matters were too im-

portant to farm out. Blade and Libby were enough.
He didn't need the added worry of a wife, then, in
the near future, another family to care for and angst
over. Concerns over running a multimillion-dollar
business were easier to handle than a crisis or
tragedy involving kin.

Before the breakdown of communication three
days ago, he'd thought he and Donna had come
close to an understanding. Together they could
share the good times without the complications.

He wanted her to understand, but the perfect
words wouldn't come.

He held her eyes with his. "I want you to be part
of my life."

She looked at him with genuine pity. "A narcis-
sistic comment if ever I heard one."

His touch trailed her red skirt's seam. "Don't
pretend you don't want me, too." Their chemistry
was through the rafters. Even here, now, he grew hot.

His hand was on her thigh before she stopped him.

"I might want a million-dollar necklace," she told
him, "but I don't break the shop window to get it."

"We don't have to be bad for each other." He
wound her hand around his and squeezed. "After
this court hearing is over—"

"What? We'll continue to sleep together and live
happily ever after?"

Her lifeless tone and glistening eyes made him think.

Who made rulings on what constituted a fairy-tale ending? His idea was two people who needed each other, every day, every night. God knows, he and Donna could make each other happy.

She disengaged her hand and bumped against him. "I have to get to work."

He eased out from the booth. "I'll drive you."

"Do me a favor." She collected her sunglasses and slid out, too. "Don't do me any favors."

Her phone rang from inside her handbag. All thumbs, she rummaged inside and stabbed the cell phone button too late. She studied the ID screen and cursed, then cursed again.

Not difficult to guess: Cruella De Vil.

Straightening his tie, he schooled his features. "Did you meet with deWalters yesterday as planned?"

He'd put money down that Maeve had got the days mixed up again. Witch.

Donna snapped her cell shut. "That's privileged information."

He didn't like her around that woman. Concern or control, didn't matter what you called it—he simply knew what he knew. When the lid blew he didn't want Donna drenched by the fallout.

He slipped a bill from his wallet and set it under

the rose vase. "How much do you need toward the maintenance costs for your project?" The wallet slid back into his jacket's breast pocket. "I haven't made my donation yet."

"I don't want your bribes. Stay away from me and my project, and that includes its benefactors."

Tate's jaw shifted.

He couldn't do either.

He collected the newspaper, slotted it under his arm and followed her to the door. She went left—sexy red heels clicking on the pavement—and he eventually went right.

For the next half an hour, he paced his office like a caged tiger. By the time he opened his private locked cabinet, his head was pounding.

Don't get emotional, think with your head.

Carefully he drew out two files, one marked Blade/Donna, the other deWalters. After a deep breath, he crossed to his desk and picked up the phone.

Donna would soon find out…this time he *would* go through with it.

Ten

Laughing, Donna threw her arms around Libby and held on tight. How wonderful to see her again and so soon. When she and Tate had their big bust-up last week, she'd been determined not to let this renewed friendship with the younger woman lapse. As it turned out, Libby had the same idea.

Tate's sister drew back, her pretty face bright and violet eyes thankful. "Are you sure you can spare the time? Buying furniture for my new apartment isn't exactly urgent business."

Cheerful for the first time in days, Donna linked an arm around Libby's waist and walked beside her into the enormous furniture retail outlet, which on the day before Christmas Eve was decorated with festoons of tinsel and silver holiday bells.

"I'd love to help." She surveyed the orderly displays of dining suites, lounges and beds, interspersed with festive trees draped in blinking lights. "Are we going ultra contemporary?"

"I'm not sure what I want yet. Everything's a little up in the air." Libby chewed her lip. "No surprise, but Tate was not too pleased by my announcement."

Holding down a deep breath, Donna continued to walk. Though she didn't want to hear about Tate, she knew Libby needed to vent. She had missed this sisterly connection, particularly now when other pieces of her life seemed to be falling apart.

Libby steered them down a wide aisle toward the dining room section. "Tate didn't take my moving out too well. I'm twenty-two, he had to know I'd leave the nest soon. But he's been so grumpy lately, what with Blade's trouble and the schedule for this new show giving him grief."

Donna's mouth twisted. The grumpy crown would fit just as well on her head. Maeve deWalters kept setting back appointments and yesterday the Registration Board had informed her that a hearing before the Professional Standards Committee was going ahead. Given she was innocent and had hidden nothing in her response to Hennessy's allegation, she could only surmise the board was being extra vigilant due to that disturbing newspaper feature.

Her cheeks flushed with embarrassment whenever she thought of it.

The night of the benefit she'd acquiesced to Tate's "request" that she interview Blade, but she'd also made it clear any assessment would be unbiased. Had he shown some muscle by organizing a hint of what was in store should she continue to hold out? But if that were true, surely he would admit that he'd somehow prompted the newspaper article. Or maybe she'd been right and he'd meant to confuse her.

Oh, hell, she'd been so angry and upset and tired of being pushed and pulled, she didn't know what to believe anymore.

Libby stopped by a chiseled stone dining table with a gold wire reindeer centerpiece. Looking coy, she ran her finger along the rectangular glass top. "Do you want to talk about it? I've heard it helps."

Donna was taken aback. "Talk about what?"

"If I had one guess why you're so preoccupied, it'd have to be over my big brother. Am I right?"

Donna strolled around her. "No."

But that was a lie. He hadn't phoned since that day at the café and she hadn't contacted him. A clean break was exactly what she'd wanted. Yet every night she found herself tossing and turning, reliving in her mind those three sensational nights with Tate. She could smell mango and briny air even now. If she closed her eyes, she could feel his hard-muscled body sliding against hers.

Libby hooked her French-manicured fingers over a chair back. "Don't make the same mistake Tate does. I'm not a child. Maybe I can help."

Donna paused. Libby may not be seventeen anymore, however, blood was said to be thicker than water. She'd like to have that much faith in her friend, but could any member of the Bridges family be trusted with such a confidence?

Libby rounded the chair and sat down. "You helped me so much when I needed you. Maybe there's something I can do for you now. Let me try." She extended her hand. "Please."

Oh, hell. She did need someone to talk to. Desperately. She couldn't talk to colleagues. None of her current friends even knew about Tate. And Libby did know everything…or almost.

Crumbling, Donna sat down, too. "Your brother and I…" Her throat convulsed and she swallowed. "Well, we've been seeing each other again."

Libby was quiet for a long, thoughtful moment. She looped a fall of sable hair behind an ear. "I

presume when you say *seeing,* there's more to it
than that."

Beneath the crush of guilt, Donna exhaled. "More
is right and, for so many reasons, I need it to end."

"Because of the conflict of interest with Blade's
assessment?"

"I told Tate a week ago to find someone else."

Libby's brows jumped. "Brave girl."

That pretty much said it all.

"Tate is just so wrong for me."

Wrong for any woman who didn't want to be
dominated by a strong male.

Libby leaned forward to take both of Donna's
hands. "Tate's a good man. He just has a hard time
understanding that doing the best by those he loves
doesn't mean he gets to rule their lives. My brother
doesn't like making mistakes, and he can't stand the
thought of anyone he cares about suffering for a
mistake, either." She shrugged. "He tries to fix
things so we don't have to."

Donna had to smile. Tate's flaws sounded justi-
fiable coming from Libby's forgiving mouth. But
the sad truth was Tate didn't listen. He simply did
what he deemed necessary and no one else's
opinions mattered.

From her perspective, that just didn't work. "Tate
needs someone who is willing to have all their deci-

sions made for them." And their feelings disregarded in the process. "There are women who would gladly hand over the reins to a powerful, attractive man."

But not her. She wanted to feel safe, not manipulated.

Libby seemed to choose her words carefully. "I don't think Tate wants any other woman."

"Give him a few days."

"He hasn't had a serious relationship since you two broke up."

Eyes burning, Donna dropped her gaze. This was harder than she'd thought. "I appreciate it, Libby, but you really don't have to try to make me feel better."

"It's true!"

Donna clenched her jaw, but in the end she couldn't hold it back. That horrible secret had been bottled up so long, she felt set to burst.

She willed her chin not to tremble. "I saw Tate kissing another woman less than a month after we broke up." After that heartbreaking night when he'd left her all alone to face their concerned guests.

Libby's brow buckled before her eyes went wide. "Oh, Lord, you must mean Madison, that personal assistant."

"I don't know who the woman was. I only know

I saw the two of them, lips locked, in his car out front of your house."

The corners of Libby's mouth tipped up. "You'd come back to make up with him?"

Hell, why not be totally honest and finally say the words aloud?

"I told myself I came over to see that you were all right. But that was only half of it." She felt her stomach twist. "I was weak." And, man oh man, had she been stupid.

Libby was shaking her head. "Tate never dated that woman. Madison was a gold digger. She kept inviting herself over for so-called business dinners. She made it well-known, even in front of me, that if Tate was available so was she. She must have tackled him in the car. I wouldn't put it past her. I remember he fired her. He didn't say why, but Blade and I knew."

The surrounding noise and bustle receded into nothing. Donna's ears began to ring. Libby was telling the truth, that much was obvious.

All these years, she'd believed it had been "out with the old and in with the new." That he'd found another woman within weeks of their breakup. What else had she been wrong about?

Libby unfolded to her feet. "I'm leaving with friends tomorrow for two weeks in Bali. Blade's holed up with Kristin somewhere." One fine eye-brow arched. "I'm thinking Tate could use some company."

A whisper-thin glimmer of hope struggled through the dark. But a past misinterpretation didn't pardon Tate's current frame of mind: basically he had coerced her into doing Blade's assessment. Then he'd manipulated the situation and her feelings in order to sleep with her. But maybe he'd already had his fill. "He hasn't called once in over a week."

Libby inclined her head. "My bet is that he's—to use his word—*regrouping.*"

"Or flat out finding a replacement for Blade's assessment as well as for his own bed." Donna cringed. "Sorry, you didn't need to hear that."

"I'm sure that's not it." Libby's expression deepened. "My brother is stubborn and has real trouble accepting that he can't keep us wrapped in cotton wool, but that failing comes from a very good place. I think he needs you to help him dig that good place out."

Wishful thinking or wise words?

Donna leveled her friend a look. "How old are you again?"

"Old enough," Libby laughed, "and anytime now Tate will have to accept it."

For the remainder of the afternoon, Donna tried

to concentrate on furniture, but facts kept rolling around in her head.

She was off Blade's case and free from the ethical dilemma. Tate hadn't fallen for the next blonde who had sashayed into his life after their broken engagement. No evidence supported her belief that he had leaked information about Hennessy's complaint.

But the biggest problem remained. Tate's king-of-all bearing. The I-know-what's-best-so-don't-bother-asking attitude. No getting around the fact that he had threatened to expose a weakness, even if initially he'd bought the rights to that story to help not harm.

Perhaps if she tried to put the past behind them…if she gave Tate this one last chance…if she completely opened her heart to him and dug really deep…

Perhaps.

Eleven

Tate's front door chimed, resulting in an entire chorus of "Jingle Bells" booming through the empty corridors of his house.

How had Libby talked him into that?

Camped out behind his study desk, he ran an eye over the script he'd worked on most the afternoon. He'd been in "the zone"; he did not appreciate being yanked out.

Buttoning the bottom half of his white collared shirt, leaving the tails hanging, he studied the title. *Good Deeds or Tainted Trust.* Not bad. A "sensational" edge. Alliteration helped. He had a couple more weeks to get everything right, but no longer than that. The show's preproduction was way behind schedule, and this series of stories was a leading contributor to the delay.

He'd procrastinated long enough.

On his way to the front door, the bell rang again. Cursing, he picked up pace.

The housekeeper was off visiting. Blade was happy someplace with Kristin. Libby was on a plane bound for Bali. God, he hoped she put locks on her suitcases.

He could think of only one person he wished to see and he hadn't worked out the best way to make that happen, particularly when a truckload of mud was about to hit an industrial-size fan.

Ruffling a hand through his hair, he swung the door open. Surprise and instant arousal struck with simultaneous brute force.

Looking fragile, Donna smiled and cleared her throat. "I, um, heard you were alone tonight so I thought I'd drop in."

With a bottle of champagne, no less.

Breathing again, Tate opened the heavy door wider. Her long, tanned legs were bare beneath her short pink dress. One of her manicured feet, in flat white sandals, stood slightly pigeon-toed. Sweet Lord, she looked delectable.

His racing desire struck a pothole. If she knew what he was working on, she'd likely smash that bottle over his skull. And he couldn't keep it from her forever.

One sandaled foot edged back. "If you're busy…"

Snapping out of his stupor, he moved forward to thread an arm around her shoulders. Her golden tan from their weekend away still glowed.

He guided her into the foyer. "I'm not busy." Not anymore. "Let me take that."

Only slightly hesitant at the intimate contact, she handed over the bottle and rubbed her hands down her dress. Her big eyes blinked as if she had something to confess. He'd keep his own confession for much later.

Closing his fingers around hers, he drew her down the wide hallway toward his private sitting room.

A smile lifted one corner of his mouth. "I didn't expect to see you."

She almost met his eyes. "We're both without family this year so it seemed…right."

Tate nodded. This time of year he missed his parents most. He'd often wondered what it must be like to have no memories of family at Christmas— or anytime, for that matter. Was it similar to never tasting chocolate and therefore never missing the treat? Or more like being deprived of food and being aware every day that you were starving? If anyone had the answer, Donna did.

She'd only spoken of her time in foster care once. Libby, Blade and a couple of their friends had seemed most interested. Donna was still unaware of how her recollections that day had unwittingly contributed to Blade's trouble on their engagement party night. Better now it should stay that way.

He led her into the salon with its own wet bar and marble fireplace, though summer Down Under was no time to build crackling hearths. He switched on the low-voltage downlights to take an edge off the shadows. Crossing to the room's far side, he opened up the full-length concertina glass doors and invited in the night air and a panoramic frame of twinkling dark velvet sky. Then he left her standing, hands laced in front, while he moved to the bar to uncork and pour the champagne.

He returned to her side, he paused to inhale her rose-petal scent, then pressed the flute into her shaky hand. He focused on her parted lips as he sipped before finally speaking. "I take it you're over your suspicion."

Her mouth was pressed tight. "Tell me one more time you had nothing to do with that newspaper article."

The hopeful tone of her voice jacked up his pulse

rate. He wanted to close his eyes and run his tongue around her mouth till he could taste her right down to his toes.

Instead, to appease her, he repeated, "I had nothing to do with that story. But you already know that, or you wouldn't be here."

"Actually this was Libby's idea," she said. "I spent yesterday afternoon helping your sister choose furniture for her new place. Seems your little chick has flown the coop."

Nonplussed, he shook his head. "Libby has her job and part-time university. Living here, she doesn't need to worry about paying bills or maintaining her car or cooking or laundry—"

"I think she's looking forward to experiencing all of those things. There comes a time in every person's life when they need to leave and a parent has to let go."

He studied her—so knowledgeable, yet she had no firsthand experience of being a parent, or of knowing her own. Driving the family bus wasn't nearly as easy as some made out. Donna would realize that when she had children of her own.

Chest catching, Tate shook off that left-field thought and moved slightly away from her.

She followed. "So Blade is still hiding out somewhere with Kristin?"

Should he sit on the couch or be far less subtle? They both knew why she'd come. The champagne was good but having her legs coiled around his hips was going to be far better.

In the soft glow, he made himself comfortable sitting on the plush white rug, one arm resting on a raised knee, the other arm propped behind. "Blade hasn't told me where they're staying. He wants complete privacy, away from media spotlights, to see if they can figure out where to go from here."

"Is he okay with your barrister arranging another psychologist for his assessment?"

"More than happy. In fact, he was insistent." When her eyebrows nudged together, he explained. "I came clean about our Queensland jaunt. That I'd organized everything and you, more or less, had little choice but to come along for the ride."

Her smile was curious. "Sounds as if you're developing a conscience."

He'd developed a conscience years ago. That had been the start of his problems.

Still standing, she swallowed more champagne. "I hope everything works out for him."

Tate was certain the assault charges the cameraman from that opposition network that had brought against Blade were garbage. Still, knowing the legal system, the outcome of Blade's day in court would be hard to call. Staying out of jail seemed all the more important to him now that Kristin was back in his life.

Tate scowled. "He'd have a better chance if Cruella deWalters could keep her big beak out of things."

Donna swirled her glass and grinned. "Cute nickname."

Not cute; fitting.

With a tilt of his chin he indicated she should join him. "Have you finalized any agreements with dear Maeve?"

Donna hesitated then carefully eased down beside him, half an arm's length away. "Not yet."

"Maybe she won't commit." He set his glass down.

"Don't say that. I understand the full history between you all now, and I sympathize. But her financial support and name are vital to my project. No one else has come forward to offer that level of assistance."

He had—at least offhandedly that day in the cafe. And maybe that was still an option. If she was still speaking to him in a month's time.

He moved closer to her, then asked, "When do you need Maeve's pledge?"

"By the end of January."

Just before ratings season kicked off. But tonight he'd forget about work.

Knowing he wasn't the only one wanting to put an end to the anticipation, he eased the glass from Donna's hand and set it beside his own. He brushed her cheek with the back of his hand before moving lower to caress her breast. He angled his head and lightly kissed her lips.

She moaned softly against his mouth before she slowly drew away.

"Tate, I won't pretend. I want to be with you again, so much. But we need to talk first...about us...our future."

He grinned. "I'm interested in what's happening now."

He kissed her again and the satisfaction of her response spread like wildfire within him, sparking the urge to skip foreplay and take her without delay.

When their lips parted, her gaze had lost three parts of its determination. "We should talk."

He tasted the slope of her jaw then growled close to her cheek. "I can't forget those nights we spent together in Queensland. Can you?"

She sighed. "I'm here, aren't I? But I need to sort out what happens next."

So he did.

His tongue trailed down her throat. "So am I moving too fast?"

She noticeably shivered before she sighed again

and, finally giving in, slanted her head to allow better access. "Always."

The rug was soft, the lights low, no one would interrupt. He braced her back and, tipping his weight, eased her down.

"I've missed you."

So damn much. Thank God tomorrow was a holiday. He hoped it rained so they could lose themselves amongst the bedclothes clear through into Boxing Day.

She craned to meet his mouth at the same time her hands moved beneath the open vee of his shirt. When he deepened the kiss and her fingers clutched and stroked his chest, a strained shirt button popped. Fever growing, he grabbed one side and tore the shirt fully open. Bunching a handful of her dress, he wrangled with it until the cotton came off over her head.

His erection throbbed against his zipper at the sight of her, sans bra, her tiny pink panties so sexy he could almost leave them on.

He cupped her breast and lovingly looped the beaded peak with the tip of his tongue. She moved beneath him, holding his head with one hand, shucking the shirt from his right shoulder with the other.

"I want to be here with you like this," she

murmured in the throaty voice he adored. "But you have to know...I need more."

His tongue stilled before finding its rhythm again. He moved his palm down her belly, beneath the pink lace triangle, between her warm thighs.

"Need more what?" His teeth grazed her nipple.

On a soft groan, she massaged his hair. "More than sex."

Hearing that word leave her mouth shot a double-barrel blast of desire through this system. Pushing off on one elbow and a knee, he found his feet, unzipped and discarded his blue jeans.

His voice deepened. "How much more?"

Her slender throat bobbed as she swallowed. Her gaze lingered before climbing to connect with his. "Maybe more than you're prepared give."

He knew where this was leading and why she was saying it now. Commitment. She'd more than implied that was the last thing she wanted from him, yet it was abundantly clear tonight that she did. But they'd gone down that path years ago and it had ended unhappily. This time he wanted to keep their relationship uncomplicated, without discussions about wedding bells and, later, diapers. He had all the responsibility he could handle with Blade, Libby and the network. He did not want more. But he did very much want this. Donna, here in his arms.

After grabbing some silk cushions off the couch, he joined her again. She rolled in and nuzzled against his chest. Taking her hand, he molded her fingers around his shaft. As she stroked and mind-blowing sensations multiplied and grew, he held her tight and admitted, "I'd give you everything if I could."

Locking her leg over his, she tilted her face and kissed him with such meaning, he couldn't help but be shamed by his past treatment of her. He hadn't wanted to use pressure the night of the benefit. He hadn't wanted to put other considerations before her feelings, now or in the past.

When her mouth broke gently away, her nose rubbed the tip of his. "What about love?" Her question reached down and twisted in his chest. "Do you love me, Tate?"

He eased her hand aside and pulled her panties down and off her legs. Positioning them face-to-face, he eased into her. As she arched beneath him, he trailed fingertips down her cheek, his mouth sampling her texture and scent in their wake.

Donna was the only woman who could make him forget all the headaches milling around outside—Libby leaving, Blade's trouble, the new show, deWalters and her scams. But he still had sense enough…

Confessions of love now might lead to promises he couldn't keep.

She locked her left arm under his right and trailed her fingers up and down his back. "You told me once you loved me."

Frowning, he increased his rhythm.

His feelings were different now. More intense, perhaps, yet...changed. He was certain of nothing except the taste of her, the feel...the heat she swaddled around his entire being.

Lightning flashed hot through his veins. Breaking the kiss, he bit down hard. Filling his lungs, he clenched every muscle around the maddening, luscious need to explode.

"I want you in my life," he repeated.

"Enough to try again?"

As she whispered in his ear, he finally gave in to the urge and let go. Pinpricks of light converged in his head then zapped through his bloodstream. As the tsunami surged, he gathered her up and spilled into her; felt her come along with him.

When the colors faded from his mind and his surroundings began to materialize again, he had only two thoughts. One, that had been a remarkable orgasm, and two, "I didn't use a condom."

Twelve

Donna was gradually floating back to reality when she heard Tate's words. Cuddling into his toned chest, she opened her eyes to find Tate's face blank with shock.

He searched her face. "I've always used protection. I've never forgotten before."

Her finger stroked his chin's raspy cleft. "I arrived out of the blue. It happened quickly."

Actually their arousal had been meteoric. Undeniable. Even now, she couldn't get close enough.

His face darkened. "That's no excuse. Are you protected?"

She shook her head. "Sorry."

But at this point in her cycle, it was unlikely she would conceive. And yet...

Although she'd had no intention of having un-protected sex tonight, now that it had happened one couldn't deny the idea of being pregnant with Tate's child had its appeal. She was twenty-eight. Tate would be her only lover; no one could overshadow or replace him. She wanted a family. God, she'd wanted that for as long as she could remember.

But he hadn't answered her question. Was it possible to overcome their difficulties and really try again? Get married? Have that family?

Brows knitted, he rolled to partially hover over her. His ocean-blue eyes infiltrated her soul. "I'm sorry."

At his gruff apology, her throat closed off. She guessed that reply in part answered her question. Clearly he was nowhere near as sorry for her as he was for himself.

Edging away, she grabbed his shirt and kept her voice light. "It's a shared responsibility, Tate. As much my fault as yours."

He'd lifted her to such heights so quickly that she hadn't considered protection. For the first time ever, they had slept together as a husband and wife would, a couple who felt sheltered by each other and wanted children. Ultimately that's what two people who felt this way were meant to do—marry, have a family. But Tate, it seemed, wasn't so sure.

Her mind spinning, she absently slotted her arms through his shirt. The lower buttons were missing. Still glowing warm inside, she wrapped the fabric around her middle.

Her focus landed on the tranquil nativity scene set out beneath a miniature Christmas tree on the mantel.

She eased to her feet. He was so quiet. She sensed the tension reeling off him.

Her fingertips trailed the tiny barn roof. "Do you want me to go?"

His graveled voice came from behind. "Of course not. I'm just…getting my breath."

Collecting the miniature manger, she inspected the swaddled baby inside. An intense sense of destiny built then washed over her. If she were pregnant, how would Tate react? Faced with the reality, surely he would come around.

Although he was overly diligent and, yes, frustratingly arrogant in some ways, no one could say he wasn't a conscientious substitute father. But Blade and even Libby were finding their own ways now. With them living their lives, Tate should feel free to concentrate on his. If he were to become a real father, wouldn't he naturally put her and their baby first?

Donna sighed and replaced the manger.

Oh, her imagination had run away. Chances were she wasn't pregnant, but at least she knew she was ready.

If Tate asked her to marry him again.

She turned to him and realized she needed a minute on her own. "Can I use the bathroom?"

Back in jeans, he finger-combed his hair and joined her. With his hand on her shoulder he pressed a kiss to her temple. "Is there something we should do? There's an all-night chemist down the road. Don't they have a morning-after pill now?"

The flush—hurt laced with irritation—doused her body. Weaving the shirt protectively around her waist, she hugged herself. "I don't know." She didn't care to discuss it. "Do they?"

"Maybe we should jump in the car and—"

Dodging his attempt to caress her, she moved toward the bathroom.

"It only takes once, Donna."

"Not at this time of the month." She bit down against rising emotion. *Don't worry, Tate. You're safe.*

His voice was husky, low. "We'll find out for sure soon, then."

Yes, they'd find out soon and only one of them would get what they wanted. Usually that was Tate.

* * *

Christmas day, she woke in Tate's bed, wrapped securely in his big protective arms.

Before she had time to reflect on her mixed feelings from the night before, he reached for the side table and presented her with an exquisite bottle of French perfume tied with gold ribbon. Taken aback, she blinked away happy tears, unraveled the ribbon and sprayed the subtle floral fragrance in her hair.

Coming close, he murmured that he'd known it would suit her perfectly. And he wouldn't hear of her feeling bad over not having a gift for him; he had all he wanted this Christmas.

Despite the faint undercurrent of unease—his concern over their forgetfulness the night before— it was the best Christmas she'd ever known. Just the two of them, all day, all night, with a fridge full of holiday food and lazy hours spent by the pool, then in bed.

The dream didn't last nearly long enough.

By midweek he was back at the office, but with Libby overseas and Blade still with Kristin, when they came together in the evenings, the time was their own. Yet every time she tried to bring up the question of their future, he would change the subject, usually kissing her until she forgot everything but the pleasure of his mouth on her body. Clearly he was avoiding the issue. Although there were times when Donna was convinced she ought to, she couldn't find the wherewithal to push the point.

Early in the new year, however, her happy bubble burst. For better or worse, she knew Tate's would, too. The board was going ahead with the investigation against her, but that was only the start.

Stomach in knots, Donna arrived late-morning at his office. His assistant informed her that Tate was downstairs preparing for an edit session. After riding the lift, she tracked Tate down to an editing booth. Through the small square glass, she saw he was alone, sitting before a panel of hi-tech equipment and monitors, absorbed in his notes. Preparing her speech, stomach twisting more, she was about to enter when Blade rushed past down the hall, obviously without seeing her.

Her smile was thoughtful.

Once she'd harbored so much anger toward Tate's brother. She'd blamed Blade for their breakup, although she could admit now that final night was a bomb that had been ticking at the end of a long-lit fuse. She hoped for both Blade and Kristin's sakes he would be found innocent of the assault charges that had been brought against him when he'd been harassed by the media and had shoved an overzealous cameraman out of his way. Everyone deserved happiness.

Putting Blade's indiscretions out of mind, she filled her lungs and swung open the door. Tate's frown as he peered up from his notes dissipated before returning with a vengeance. Eyes suddenly dark and eyebrows slashed together, he pushed aside his notes, leapt from his seat and stood before her, hands locked eye level on either side on the jamb.

His grin seemed strained "Hey, what are you doing here?"

She blinked several times. She wasn't imagining his agitation. Maybe she should wait until tonight. But she couldn't.

Easing back her shoulders, she tried on a teasing smile. "No kiss hello?"

He dotted a welcome on her cheek as his hands dropped and he spun her around. "We'll get out of this stuffy booth and have a coffee."

His words were clipped, his expression…almost guilty. Then she saw the image, in triplicate, on the editing screens.

A withering, dizzy sensation came over her. Digging her heels in, she skirted around Tate and stared, gaping, at the monitors. Her voice all but lost, she pointed a finger at the screens.

"What's Maeve deWalters doing up there?"

Maeve's bright red hair was as elaborately coiffed as ever. The shot looked like a recent portrait had been freeze-framed and captured behind a mock-up of crude jail bars.

From the doorway, Tate exhaled heavily then cursed under his breath. "Well, you had to learn sometime."

As nausea rose and damp prickled across her forehead, she inched around. "Learn what?"

One stride and he crossed the space between them. He held her shoulders with branding hands as he seemed to will her to remain calm.

Her legs felt boneless. If he hadn't been holding her, she'd have fallen in a pile. The life force seemed to drain from her, along with every ounce of belief she'd ever had in him.

In them.

"You're really going to do it, aren't you?" she asked over the lump in her throat. "You're going to do a story on Maeve and maybe destroy me in the process. I suppose you have the Hennessy story lined up next."

Hunching over her, Tate's fingers dug into her arms. "I'm not trying to destroy you. I'm trying to *save* you."

"Then why didn't you have the decency to tell me instead of letting me find out like this?"

"I tried to tell you."

He meant the conversation that night in the bungalow? "You said you thought Maeve was corrupt. That I'd do better to look elsewhere for support. You didn't say you had hard evidence and were taking a deep breath, getting ready to shout it to the world."

"It's high time someone did. Maeve deWalters was well on her way to being crooked when my parents died. These days her financial advisor and offshore bank accounts help make the funneling of funds so much easier."

She crossed her arms. "What evidence do you have?"

"Enough, and from a reliable source. But I have to keep this quiet. The release needs to be timed well for two reasons."

"The first would somehow revolve around your need for revenge."

He ignored her gibe aimed at the role Maeve deWalters had played in his parents deaths. "This is part of my job. Hard journalism is what this show's about. This story will come out either way. Question is, do we air it first or will somebody else get the privilege?"

Years of frustration and hurt swelled inside her chest. The ache was so great she thought she might burst.

"Then I suppose congratulations are in order. Too bad I get trampled along the way."

She'd mistakenly assumed that if Blade and Libby relied on themselves, Tate would be left to focus on their life as a couple. She'd thought he would have time for her now—that he would naturally consider her feelings.

She'd forgotten about his work. Her feelings would always come second to his precious television network.

Her vision blurred with brimming tears. "You haven't changed."

She'd hoped that her love could transform him. That was just wishful thinking. One person couldn't change another, she knew that better than most, yet the exhilaration of being close to him again had left her blind. Her love for Tate wouldn't change him. Nothing would.

Not even a child.

His chin edged up. "I have a duty to the public. I can't sit on this or sweep it under a mat."

"I understand you're on a timeline. Can't have the King beaten at the post now, can we?"

He growled out an impatient breath. "You're lining up to sign with Maeve. Auctions, dinners, special events. After she takes her cut, I doubt a third of the contributions would make it to your project."

He honestly didn't see. "This isn't about whether Maeve deWalters is corrupt. I'm upset because you had no intention of discussing this story with me until after it had aired. You go straight ahead and do what *you* think is right, and I'm supposed to forgive you after the fact. But even if I didn't like what I heard, I deserved to know about this story."

He continually took for granted that she would accept being kept in the dark and looking like a fool to boot. Never again.

He cursed under his breath and rushed a hand through his hair. "I was going to tell you about this story. I just needed…the right moment."

"It's a little late," she blurted out. "Maeve and I worked out details this morning, right before I received a message from the board to attend a meeting tomorrow. I assume the Hennessy investigation is going ahead."

Tate froze then trailed a weary hand through his hair again. While she trembled, she imagined his mind ticking over.

"All right," he said. "First things first. Maeve. You don't want your name linked in any way with hers. The taxation and other departments will run fine-tooth combs through her books and anyone associated with her. We'll see my lawyer, get you out of this. I'll fix it."

The booth extension rang. Tate looked at it, back at her then snapped up the receiver. Donna couldn't help but smile at the irony—commanding, arrogant and predictable to the end. The third worst day of her life and still Tate couldn't let a phone ring.

"Bridges here." His square jaw tightened. "Put her through." His attention landed on Donna. "I was expecting this call from Bali. Libby left a message a half hour ago. Molly said she sounded worried. If she's somehow landed herself in trouble with the Indonesian authorities, I need to know."

Donna didn't have time to wonder whether Libby was in some kind of trouble before Tate covered the mouthpiece with a palm. "I thought you might have some other news," he hesitated, "about the other night."

What he meant was—*about the mistake*. When they'd loved each other so well, so completely, protection had totally slipped both their minds. Yes, indeed, she'd come to see him about that, too.

His brow creased as he studied her face. "You've found out?" His expression said, *I'm here for you.* But beneath the concern she read more clearly, *I'll fix it.*

Her answering grin felt cut from dry ice. Just eleven days had passed since that night when she'd told him it was late in her cycle and not to worry. But three home tests conducted on separate days confirmed suspicions. She was late. She was pregnant. She was sure.

She slanted her head and manufactured a dismissive face. "All clear. Nothing to worry about."

Nothing you want to hear or concern yourself with.

He closed his eyes and exhaled as if to say "Thank God" a moment before he had the receiver more firmly to his ear. "Libby—that you? What's wrong?"

When his tone leveled and she was certain Libby was all right—it sounded as if she only wanted to stay another week—Donna walked out.

She felt numb inside, more alone and vulnerable than at any time in her life. Nothing Tate said—no mortal thing he could do—would make a difference now. He'd hinted that day at the café that he would make a donation to her safe house project. It killed her to ever think it, but right now she would almost rather her project fail than be beholden to him. She'd held her heart out to him and he'd robbed her of everything.

Well…not *everything.*

Thirteen

Tate watched Donna turn and just missed catching her arm as she left the booth.

Damn! They were nowhere near finished their conversation. On top of this deWalters mess, Donna had just told him she wasn't pregnant. After days of wondering, he now knew she wasn't carrying his child…

"Libby, if everything is okay, I need to go. I'll see you in a week."

His little sister was all grown up and making her own decisions. Right now he had enough on his plate sorting out his own life.

On the other end of the line, Libby's voice

sounded concerned. "Is something wrong? Everything okay between you and Donna?"

"It will be."

Although, given the gutted look on Donna's face just now, maybe he was kidding himself. Had he lost her for good this time?

He hung up. Two strides put him at the doorway, but Blade appeared out of nowhere to block his path.

His brother held up two hands. "Whoa! Where's the fire?"

Tate sidled out the door. "I'll explain later." He needed to catch Donna before she left the building.

"Sure. Just thought you might like to know our barrister called."

Tate stopped and turned. "What's the problem now?"

"No problem." Blade crossed his arms and rocked on his heels. "I'm a free man! The prosecution withdrew the charges. Must have seen they couldn't prove their case and didn't want to waste any more time or money."

"Thank God that's over." He'd always known there was no real case.

Never again did he want that kind of worry, and he was certain Blade wouldn't create it. A rare kind of peace seemed to glow from his brother since

Blade and Kristin had begun dating again. Tate prayed it would work out for them and the world would leave them the hell alone.

Blade slapped Tate on the arm as he passed. "I'm off to celebrate with my girl."

Tate rotated to watch his brother amble down the corridor. "We've got a busy day ahead."

As soon as he finished speaking with Donna, he had to get back to it. He was up to his eyeballs. He had no choice, and he needed Blade's help.

Blade edged around. "Mate, I love my job but I love my lady more. We have our life back. If that's not worth taking the afternoon off, I don't know what is. You must feel the same now you and Donna are an item again." Lifting his chin to loosen his tie, Blade looked around. "Could've sworn I saw her around earlier." He seemed concerned now. "Everything okay in lovers' lane?"

A phrase was still resonating through Tate's brain—*I love my lady more*—when he snapped back and waved his brother off. "Fine. Everything's great. You go."

"Might see you tomorrow then." With a curious look, Blade headed off again.

"I'll be here." Like every other day, even most weekends, although he had enjoyed that brilliant seasonal interlude. Having Donna snuggled up or laughing beside him over Christmas break had left him feeling more refreshed, more himself, than he had in years.

Oh, God. *Donna.*

He strode back into the booth and dialed reception. Apparently Donna had just walked out of the front exit. The receptionist had seen her jump into a cab. Dropping the receiver back in its cradle, he glanced up to see Maeve's hideous face and teased red hair blasting out at him from the monitors.

Welcome to the rest of your week.

He set his hands on the back of the seat as his mind filled with a montage of other images—his parents hugging him goodbye, Blade waving goodbye, Libby saying goodbye, Donna meaning good—

The images imploded and he slammed the chair against the desk.

Donna was right, and wrong. He did want revenge on Maeve deWalters; he longed to see that witch behind bars where she belonged. And he also wanted to keep Donna safe from Maeve's influence, but without any unpleasant scenes beforehand or the chance of Maeve being tipped off before everything was set to go. To his mind, if he aired this story without Donna's prior knowledge, she would simply have to see reason and accept that he'd had no alternative. Then again…

He thought the same way on their engagement party night, as well as all those other times he'd let Donna down because he'd been convinced she would understand about priorities, which often meant his siblings or his work. It was no secret that he liked things done his way.

But when all was said and done, why should Donna understand or accept how he'd gone about this? She'd said he hadn't changed. He wouldn't disagree that his habit of acting first, talking later, could be labeled as arrogance. He was paying for that today. Fate had handed him a second chance with Donna. But in trying to control the agenda yet again, had he blown whatever future they might have had together?

He surveyed the claustrophobic booth.

This was the sum of his adult life. Trying to make it up to Blade and Libby, trying to appease his conscience, and for what? Gratitude? Admiration? Or for absolution and the privilege of returning home to a huge empty house each evening, and for what? When did it end?

Visualizing that empty house disintegrating around his ears, he moved into the corridor. People rushing to shoot a news update or hurrying tapes down to pre-production didn't register. Nothing registered but one monumental, all-encompassing mistake.

He'd tried so hard to make up for what he'd lost that given the speed with which Donna had left a moment ago, he might well have lost the one person who meant more to him than anything on the planet. He was deeply sorry his parents were gone. He loved Blade and Libby, but his work with them was pretty much done. He should feel free. Instead he felt empty. Like that house. He'd felt emptiness the moment Donna had said they wouldn't be parents.

He wouldn't be a father...

Setting his jaw, he headed down the corridor.

Who was he kidding? He couldn't work today anymore than Blade could. He needed to see Donna. He was certain she believed him about Maeve de-Walters's corruption; she knew he wouldn't risk his reputation unless he had strong facts that would stand up against scrutiny. But as she'd said, Maeve de Walters's illegal activities weren't at the heart of their problems. He had to figure out some way to make Donna trust him and assure her that he would never put her second again.

Thirty traffic-weaving minutes later, he was home and standing at the foot of his bed. Fresh on the satin quilt he smelled her scent. Bouncing off the walls he heard her laughter, but...

He spun a tight circle.

He and Donna and *here* didn't work.

Light reflecting off the side table caught his eye. He came close and softly smiled...her gold bracelet watch. Collecting the jewelry, he let the smooth links slip through each set of fingers while he worked out what was missing, how to make it right.

Unevenness beneath the watch face made him look. Etched on the gold lay the inscription he'd quoted to the engraver all those years ago before the trouble had set in. He stared at the single word and concentrated.

He needed to reclaim that time. Needed to get her back.

Forever.

Fourteen

Two days later, in an up-market suburban restaurant, Donna sat wringing her hands. Maeve deWalters was due to arrive at any moment. Though the meeting wouldn't be a pleasant one, Donna doubted it could be worse than her anguish when she'd walked out on Tate.

Rather than receding, the pain had grown worse. He hadn't pursued her, hadn't even called. Given his recent record in such matters, she guessed she shouldn't be surprised.

Heart thudding low in her chest, Donna collected

her dinner napkin and absentmindedly wound the starched linen around her fingers.

She could live without his embrace. Could live without his sexy smile. Heaven knows she *couldn't* live without her dignity. Once again Tate had placed his interests before her feelings. She didn't want to continue being Tate Bridges's mistress, but more so she couldn't live with wondering when and how he would humiliate her next.

Libby had said Tate was a good man. That he merely had a hard time understanding that doing the best by those he loved didn't mean ruling their lives. Whether or not that was true didn't matter. Bottom line was, he continued to hurt her. If she persisted in seeing him, she was condoning his behavior and had only herself to blame.

Visible through the wall-to-wall window facing the street, a dark rolling blur caught her attention. The gleaming wheels...those number plates...the gunmetal-grey paint. Pulling up at the curb outside was Tate's European convertible.

Adrenaline flooded her system.

This wasn't a coincidence. Had April told him she'd be here? Or was Maeve the person Tate had come to hunt down?

A prim voice at Donna's side made her jump.

"I must confess," Maeve said, placing her pocketbook on the table, "I'm pleased you called to arrange this meeting."

Her mind racing, Donna glanced between her company and the convertible. Tate had emerged from the driver's side, looking edible in tailored dark trousers and button-down shirt. His hair rumpled in a stiff breeze as he analyzed his surroundings, checked his watch then shut the door.

Swallowing hard, Donna looked again to Maeve. "It's about our agreement."

She needed to wrap this up quickly. Get out of here fast. The last thing she needed was Tate hurling a live grenade into the foxhole.

With a disenchanted air, Maeve eased into the tapestry-covered seat. "Precisely what I wish to discuss." She flicked a hovering waiter away then clasped her age-worn hands, and their long red tips, beneath her chin.

"I am loath to bring it up, however, I believe you've been consorting with those horrible Bridges boys." Her hazel eyes glowed. "A rather obtuse pastime, you'll agree."

In Donna's peripheral vision, she saw Tate slot his sunglasses into his shirt pocket and breeze around the building's corner, out of sight.

"How…" Donna paused, swallowed. "How did you know?"

Maeve arched an eyebrow. "Pet, you can't keep secrets from me." She sat back, not amused. "Naturally this changes our relationship."

Picturing the scene about to explode, Donna nodded. "More than you know."

His face dark, Tate stopped at the maître d's podium and Donna withered in her seat. She prayed he wouldn't turn this into a public incident.

After flinging a determined glance around, Tate strode over. Maeve had begun a speech, of which Donna had heard not a word, when he appeared by their table like a knight drawing his sword—or bringing it down.

More than ever, his dominating presence sent electric impulses hopscotching over her skin. Though she'd have done anything to prevent it, she quivered with the urge to kiss the bristled shadow of his jaw…hear the rumble of his rich voice against her ear.

"Hello, Maeve." His voice today sounded ominously deep.

The doyen's mouth stopped moving. She blinked then pivoted around. Her souring expression shrank in on itself like an apple speed drying in the sun. Finally she flicked her hand and feigned an inspection of her menu.

"Please leave. No one invited you." Accusing hazel eyes slid up to scorch Donna's. "Unless…"

Tate ignored the dismissal. "This meeting is over. Donna is unable to proceed with any agreement, verbal or otherwise."

Donna half expected a camera crew to race out. She knew how Tate's business mind worked. High-stakes confrontations such as this made for excellent promo vision. However, as much as the realization would prick his ego, this meeting was not about Tate or his precious show.

Although her breathing was anything but even, her tone was surprisingly calm. "This is none of your business, Tate."

Take your commanding good looks and insufferable sex appeal and go—just *go*.

Maeve sneered. "Are we rehearsing for one of your network's soap operas, Mr. Bridges? *Love Conquers All*, perhaps?" Eyes bright, she drummed her nails atop the menu. "I see you're as impudent as your brother."

Tate's dark eyes simmered at the slur against Blade and his—in Maeve's opinion—unwelcome attachment to Kristin. "You can hang up your broom there, Maeve. You have no power over them anymore."

A corner of Maeve's mouth ticked as her eyes narrowed to vengeful slits. She sliced her attention back to Donna. "As I said, highly obtuse." She collected her pocketbook. "I'm pulling my support as of now, and not purely due to Mr. Bridges's uncouth behavior." Her tone was one of manufactured regret. "I understand misconduct charges are being heard by your peers."

Donna's cheeks toasted more with every word. Not in humiliation but in anger.

"Actually the board has decided no disciplinary action is necessary." They'd thought it fair and reasonable to inform her in person that the complainant in question had lodged similar grievances against two other reputable professionals. All the charges had proved to be unfounded. At least one turn in these crazy few weeks had gone her way.

Tate's hand brushed her arm as his expression melted with relief. "That's great news."

Great was an understatement. Now he genuinely had nothing to hold over her head.

Smug, Maeve pushed to her feet. "We all know the saying. Where there's smoke..."

Tate nodded. "I know of at least one instance where that's true."

Donna's patience broke. "Can you both please just be quiet!" She retrieved an envelope from her bag. "Maeve, to make it official, this letter states I no longer require your support with regard to The Judith Safe House Trust."

Maeve sputtered. "You're dismissing *me?*" Her jowls wobbled. "How dare you!"

Tate stood beside Donna. "Save your energy, Maeve. You'll need every ounce soon enough."

Donna silently ended the sentence. Maeve would need her strength when the authorities caught up with her money-laundering schemes. She wondered how the redhead would do without her hairdresser in jail.

Maeve blanched. "And just what is that supposed to mean?"

"Watch the news and find out," Tate happily replied.

Running a calculating eye over them both, Maeve straightened and stormed out.

When Tate focused his full attention on her, Donna shivered in her seat. Despite everything, she glowed inside when his encouraging eyes smiled down. "You made the right choice."

As his finger curved her jaw, she longed to lean into his caress. But she wouldn't make the same mistake again. Twice was shameful enough.

She collected her bag and got to her feet. "What I did had nothing to do with you." Well, not in the way he might think. "Your problem with Maeve might have a personal origin, but you wouldn't air a story that wasn't fully grounded in fact. I'm not foolish enough to put my pride before my foundation's best interests."

She owed it to Judith as well as so many other unknown women who would one day need that shelter.

Tate tugged his ear. "I have it on good authority the story about Maeve will hit the air by the end of the week. Our news department will cover it, but unfortunately that's a little early for our debut show to compete with."

Her gullible heart contracted. "That story meant a lot to you."

He rolled back one big shoulder. "There'll be other stories."

As that edict sank in, Donna inwardly cringed. Lots and lots of other stories would always mean more to him than she did. She was through having her feelings trampled on. She needed someone who thought enough of her to discuss important issues, not a man who hogged the reins, made all the decisions and was proud of it.

Biting down to stave off the hurt, she edged past. "I have to go. Good luck, Tate."

As she moved off, she sensed him striding behind her.

"Do you have an appointment?"

At the counter, she signed her account. She set down her pen and faced him. "That's none of your concern."

"I'd like it to be."

Unwelcome arousal flashed through her, but she reached in extra deep and found her resolve. "And I'd like to keep this polite. Excuse me."

She continued on out the door and into the muggy street. Overhead, grumbling thunderclouds rolled in from the east.

Tate was by her side. "I have something to show you."

Focusing on the noisy traffic, she spotted a cab. She moved to the curb. "Not interested."

Stepping in her path, he cut her off. "Donna… I'm sorry."

Raw emotion—swift and cruel—sprang up to sting her nose and strangle her aching heart. She sighed. "Even if I believed you, Tate, don't you see? It's too late for apologies. Whatever we shared couldn't last. Obviously you don't want to make a commitment and now I don't think you should." He tried to interrupt, but she held up a hand. "You have your family and your work. That's enough for you. I'm sure you won't have any trouble finding someone else to warm your bed."

The cab pulled up. Moving around Tate, she tried to slide inside but he blocked her path.

"Do you know why Blade got into a brawl the night of our engagement party?"

Her breath caught in her chest. Why on earth was he bringing this up now?

She stretched to reach for the cab's door handle. "I don't need to know."

"That night one of Blade's friends had taken great pleasure in running your reputation down."

She heard the words but they didn't make sense. Confused, she slowly shook her head. "What are you talking about?"

Tate reached over and pounded on the cab's roof, sending it away. Then he came closer. "You remember talking about your foster care days in front of Libby, Blade and his friend during that Australia Day barbeque?"

It seemed so long ago. They'd all been laughing and sharing, and she'd felt this overwhelming need to divulge her past, to connect and feel part of their circle—their family.

She nodded. "I remember."

"Early on the evening of our engagement party, Blade's university friends were having a drink and discussing how well suited Blade and Kristin were. They agreed Maeve should've been pleased her daughter had found such a catch. Then that friend from the barbeque—"

Tate's jaw hardened, as if he were debating whether or not to go on. He lowered his voice.

"Blade's friend went over the top, spouting off about water finding its own level. How Kristin and Blade were social equals, but he couldn't see why I would be interested in you, someone who'd been dropped at the church stairs and had no background, no pedigree." Tate blinked twice. "Blade said his silver-spoon friend called you a bony lost puppy looking for a home."

She felt slightly light-headed. How cruel to hear those words aloud…and yet that's exactly how she'd felt. Though she'd never known it as clearly as this moment. She didn't belong anywhere, not then, and in many ways not even now.

Exhaling, she looked Tate in the eye. "So Blade hit him."

"I didn't condone that behavior," he told her. He took her arm and began to walk with her. "But I understood. Blade told his friend you were the kindest lady he'd ever known. How you'd told him that if ever he needed to talk to someone, you were always there."

They reached Tate's car. Facing her, he grabbed both her hands. "That boy kept ribbing Blade. On top of all the trouble with Kristin, Blade's lid popped. The boy's father was a retired cop. I had to call in some mighty big favors that night."

Donna's eyes squeezed tight. "Why didn't you tell me?"

"I put off calling you that night, hoping it would be wrapped up quickly. I was wrong. When I did phone, you didn't answer my calls. The next day you barely spoke to me, other than to say it was over. As time went on, I didn't think burdening you with those details would make a difference."

Her head was reeling. "All these years, and Blade had only acted to protect me."

But if she'd known the facts back then, would it have made a difference to her decision to stop seeing Tate? As heartrending as Tate's admission was, she couldn't be sure it would have. Tate had put his sibling and work commitments ahead of her many time before that episode. His absence that night had merely been the final straw.

There was always some sound reason behind Tate's actions. Her hurt stemmed more from his inability to see that she deserved to be treated with respect instead of being kept in the back row. She couldn't go on that way, not knowing exactly where or how she would fit in with his plans.

Tate opened his passenger door and set his warm palm on her back. "Drive with me. There's more you need to know."

Fifteen

Donna wasn't certain how far they drove. She felt the cool wind funneling through her hair, saw the heavy rolling sky above. And knew Tate, powerful in the driver's seat—speeding up, slowing down, changing gears—was, as always, fully in control. She felt anything but.

As Tate took a corner, she studied his stone-carved jaw. Ripples of stark desire, interlaced with dread, swam out from her center. She'd made some horrible mistakes. Was she making another one?

When he'd asked her along for this drive, everything inside of her had screamed no. But he'd said there was more she needed to know. In light of what she'd finally learned today, she wouldn't rest until she knew it all.

The car swerved off into a quiet dead end overlooking a deserted stretch of beach. As the tires rolled to a stop, intermittent dots of cold rain splattered on the bonnet and fell on her lap. The approaching storm's salty gusts blew icily on her arms and face.

Seconds after swinging out of the driver's side, Tate opened her door, but she hesitated taking the hand she knew as well as her own. "This isn't the best day for a stroll."

He frowned. "You're right. It's about to pour. We should find some shelter."

Before she could suggest they put up the top and leave, he folded her hand in his. As his familiar masculine heat soaked through and her defenses teetered on a cliff, he led her to a picket fence painted a holiday turquoise-blue. Without a pause, he swung open the hip-high gate.

Taking in the private landscaped gardens and the serene Queenslander-style home before them, Donna tugged back. "We don't want to bother anyone."

All species of palms rustled around the enormous three-sided verandah. There wasn't another house for miles.

"Whoever lives here obviously likes their privacy," she said, as the drops fell harder, plink-plonking on the high-pitched corrugated roof. She tugged again. "Let's get back in the car and go somewhere else."

A smile lit Tate's face as he cast an eye over the wide porch stairs and white and turquoise trimmed front door. "It looks kind of friendly to me."

A wind chime hanging above the door tinkled in the strong breeze and a delicious fruity scent filled her lungs. Behind a blossoming frangipani tree, she spied another tree laden with heavy bunches of ripe fruit.

Mangos.

When he drew her into the yard, this time her feet made the decision for her.

He indicated a slight incline decorated with a colorful garden display. "Now there's something you don't see every day."

Holding back the hair blowing over her head, Donna took in the stone sundial then read the single word created by swirls and patches of scarlet ground-cover roses. The petals, which by their decoration must have been freshly planted, seemed to grow larger and brighter the more she stared. Her heartbeat knocking at her ribs, she could do no more than breathe out the word.

"Forever."

Her gold bracelet watch…the inscription. Donna

held her stomach. But what did it mean here, today, in that windblown pretty flower bed?

Afraid to ask, but too curious not to, she looked up and searched Tate's eyes. "I don't understand."

"I was wrong, Donna. Wrong and arrogant and stupid."

The penny dropped. "This is your house, isn't it?"

"No. This is *our* house."

She bit her lip and edged away. "Please don't do this. On the surface this might look romantic, but deep down it doesn't mean anything. I know who you are and I know you can't change." Tate wasn't happy unless he was fully in charge. She couldn't deal with that anymore.

"People *must* be able to change, or you'd be out of a job."

He was twisting things. "That's different."

"It's only different because after the Maeve de-Walters episode you don't want to take another chance on me?"

"It's more complicated than that. You've proven time and again you'll do what you think is right without considering me or anyone else. In a costume drama that might be heroic, but in real life it doesn't work. You don't even respect me enough to answer whenever I've asked lately about our future. It's pretty obvious what you want from me, and it's not marriage and it certainly isn't children." Her voice caught on the final word.

He took a moment then spoke. "Blade is taking over full responsibility for the current affairs show. I signed off on it yesterday. From now on, it's his baby."

She shook her head. That show meant too much to Tate to hand over. "I don't believe you."

"In fact, Blade is now joint CEO."

She blinked several times. Tate would never surrender that much control.

He seemed to read her mind. "At first I thought it would be hard to ease back, but actually it felt so good that after I spoke to Blade, I rang Libby and promoted her out of children's production to help share the responsibility. She was thrilled. I, on the other hand, am taking an indefinite sabbatical. As of this moment, you are my main and only concern."

As much as she wanted to, Donna couldn't buy it. "If that's true, I'm happy you feel confident enough to share the network's load with your brother and sister. But if this is some kind of scheme to get me back into your bed, you're missing an important point. I don't want to continue with our affair. I will not be your on-the-side lover. Not for one day. Certainly not forever."

"Which brings me back to the flower bed." His arm wound securely around her as he walked with her up the incline. "You'll understand when you see the top half."

Quizzing his eyes, she gradually let her vision wander back to the garden. Above *Forever,* above the sundial, the flowers spelled out a question—two words that blocked her throat and flooded her body with disbelief and terrifying hope.

His deep voice rumbled gently like the thunder overhead. "Would you like me to read it for you?"

A raindrop wet the tip of her nose as, gaze glued to the display, she pressed her lips together and, speechless, nodded quickly.

Her blurred vision panned over each letter as he drew her close and murmured, "Marry me."

She turned into him, hiding her hot face against his chest. His arms immediately folded her in close.

"I bought this house yesterday," he said. "I thought we could live here together—you, me...our own little family."

The vee of his hand supported her head as his mouth lowered until his lips hovered a hair's breadth from hers. "Forgive me, Donna. Be my wife."

A tear escaped. "You want a family?"

His loving smile wrapped around her heart. "The moment I realized we hadn't used protection that night, although I wasn't ready to admit it, I think I knew. I love you, Donna. I want to build the rest of my life around you." He claimed the kiss she'd secretly ached to surrender all day.

As he pressed her close, the world dropped away and she found herself floating atop a cloud. A sparkling jet of sensation flew up from her toes, sending her giddy with desire and so much more. When he gently broke away and she felt the earth beneath her shaky legs once more, her mind cleared enough to ask again.

"You're *really* sure?"

"About a family?" He contentedly studied her face. "One hundred percent. I'm sorry I went about it the long way. Truth is…I was worried I'd disappoint you, make some fatal mistake and never be able to make it up to you. But I won't let that kind of thinking get in the way again. I want to be a part of you, to feel *complete* with you—if you'll have me."

"You want to be a parent."

He grinned. "I'm going to throw away my cell phone, moor a boat outside our door and teach my son to fish like I always wished my father had taught me."

"And if you had a daughter?"

"I'm sure a girl can learn to throw a line." He kissed her nose. "Girl or boy, one of each or more, I'll be happy."

She called upon all her courage and faith.

"That's good news, because when I said I wasn't, actually I was. Or rather, I am—" she released the word "—pregnant."

A second later, she was swept up in the cradle of his arms, twirling through the air. When he stopped, she was laughing and he looked as if he'd been given the world on a plate.

His chest expanded as he inhaled deeply. "I'm going to be a father."

She nodded.

"We're going to be a family."

Beaming, she nodded again.

Drops of falling rain clung to his lashes. "But you still haven't answered my question. Donna, I love you."

Her reply was the truest words she'd ever spoken. "I love you, too."

"Will you marry me?"

She searched his eyes. Yes, he wanted a wedding as much as she did, but his gaze told her more than that. Tate hadn't changed. He'd simply found a part of himself that he'd lost long ago—Tate before his parents' accident, before he'd felt obliged to give and be more than anyone expected. She saw that awareness shining in his eyes and knew the man who had proposed today would be the best husband and father he possibly could be.

Nevertheless, she couldn't help but tease him.

Still in his arms, she drew a lazy fingertip around his jaw. "I'll marry you on one condition."

Studying her expression, he arched an eyebrow. "I see…an ultimatum. You want my donation for your foundation? Consider it done."

She glowed inside. "Thank you. But that's not it."

His chin kicked up. "Let's have it then."

He'd played his little game. She'd play hers.

She wrinkled her nose. "I'm not sure. We're out in the open."

His smiling eyes assured her. "We're the only ones here. I promise, you're safe."

"Maybe we should go inside." She grinned. "Can I tempt you?"

Tate murmured, "Always." As the rain came down her chest, his mouth claimed hers again and Donna knew in her heart finally she was home.

* * * * *

Please look for Robyn Grady's next release,
HIRED FOR THE BOSS'S BED,
available July 2008 from
Harlequin Presents collection.

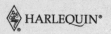

DIAMONDS DOWN UNDER

SATIN &
A SCANDALOUS AFFAIR

DIAMONDS DOWN UNDER

When Dani Hammond is hired by a mysterious
millionaire to create the ultimate piece of jewelry,
she doesn't realize her job comes with enticing
benefits—like gemologist Quinn Everard.
And Quinn isn't expecting the sparks that fly
when he meets Dani. After Dani's past resurfaces,
Quinn must decide whether to betray the woman
he has fallen for or stand by her side....

**Don't miss the next installment of
the Diamonds Down Under series—
Boardrooms & a Billionaire Heir by Paula Roe,
coming in May 2008 from Silhouette Desire!**

"Always Powerful, Passionate and Provocative"

REQUEST YOUR FREE BOOKS!

2 FREE NOVELS PLUS 2 FREE GIFTS!

Passionate, Powerful, Provocative!

YES! Please send me 2 FREE Silhouette Desire® novels and my 2 FREE gifts (gifts are worth about $10). After receiving them, if I don't wish to receive any more books, I can return the shipping statement marked "cancel". If I don't cancel, I will receive 6 brand-new novels every month and be billed just $4.05 per book in the U.S. or $4.74 per book in Canada, plus 25¢ shipping and handling per book and applicable taxes, if any*. That's a savings of almost 15% off the cover price! I understand that accepting the 2 free books and gifts places me under no obligation to buy anything. I can always return a shipment and cancel at any time. Even if I never buy another book, the two free books and gifts are mine to keep forever.

225 SDN ERVX 326 SDN ERVM

Name	(PLEASE PRINT)	
Address		Apt. #
City	State/Prov.	Zip/Postal Code

Signature (if under 18, a parent or guardian must sign)

Mail to the **Silhouette Reader Service:**
IN U.S.A.: P.O. Box 1867, Buffalo, NY 14240-1867
IN CANADA: P.O. Box 609, Fort Erie, Ontario L2A 5X3

Not valid to current subscribers of Silhouette Desire books.

Want to try two free books from another line?
Call 1-800-873-8635 or visit www.morefreebooks.com.

* Terms and prices subject to change without notice. N.Y. residents add applicable sales tax. Canadian residents will be charged applicable provincial taxes and GST. This offer is limited to one order per household. All orders subject to approval. Credit or debit balances in a customer's account(s) may be offset by any other outstanding balance owed by or to the customer. Please allow 4 to 6 weeks for delivery. Offer available while quantities last.

Your Privacy: Silhouette Books is committed to protecting your privacy. Our Privacy Policy is available online at www.eHarlequin.com or upon request from the Reader Service. From time to time we make our lists of customers available to reputable third parties who may have a product or service of interest to you. If you would prefer we not share your name and address, please check here. ☐

SDES08

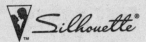

Romantic
SUSPENSE

Sparked by Danger,
Fueled by Passion.

The Taken

Tierney Doyle is used to being criticized for
her psychic abilities, yet the tough-as-nails—
and drop-dead-gorgeous—detective has no doubt
about what she has uncovered in the case of a
string of unsolved murders. And Tierney is slowly
discovering that working so close to her partner,
detective Wade Callahan, could be lethal.

Look for

Danger Signals
by Kathleen Creighton

Available in April wherever books are sold.

presents

Planning perfect weddings...
finding happy endings!

Amidst the rustle of satins and silks, the scent of red roses and white lilies and the excited chatter of brides-to-be, six friends from Boston are The Wedding Belles—they make other people's wedding dreams come true....

But are they always the wedding planner...never the bride?

Who will be the next to say "I do"?

And don't miss the exciting wedding-planner tips and author reminiscences that accompany each book!

www.eHarlequin.com

HRI7507

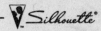
Silhouette®

SPECIAL EDITION™

Introducing a brand-new miniseries

Men of Mercy Medical

Gabe Thorne moved to Las Vegas to open a
new branch of his booming construction
business—and escape from a recent tragedy.
But when his teenage sister showed up pregnant
on his doorstep, he really had his hands full.
Luckily, in turning to Dr. Rebecca Hamilton for
the medical care his sister needed, he found
a cure for himself....

Starting with

THE MILLIONAIRE AND THE M.D.

by *TERESA SOUTHWICK,*

available in April wherever books are sold.

COMING NEXT MONTH

#1861 SATIN & A SCANDALOUS AFFAIR—
Jan Colley
Diamonds Down Under
Hired by a handsome and mysterious millionaire to design the ultimate piece of jewelry, she didn't realize her job would come with enticing fringe benefits.

#1862 MARRYING FOR KING'S MILLIONS—
Maureen Child
Kings of California
He needs a wife. She needs a fortune. But when her ex arrives at their door, their marriage of convenience might not be so binding after all.

#1863 BEDDED BY THE BILLIONAIRE—Leanne Banks
The Billionaires Club
She was carrying his late brother's baby. Honor demanded he take care of her...passion demanded he make her his own.

#1864 PREGNANT AT THE WEDDING—Sara Orwig
Platinum Grooms
Months before, they'd shared a passionate weekend. Now the wealthy playboy has returned to seduce her back into his bed... until he discovers she's pregnant with his child!

#1865 A STRANGER'S REVENGE—
Bronwyn Jameson
With no memory of their passionate affair, a business tycoon plots his revenge against the woman he believes betrayed him.

#1866 BABY ON THE BILLIONAIRE'S DOORSTEP—
Emily McKay
Was the baby left on his doorstep truly his child? Only one woman knows the truth...and only the ultimate seduction will make her tell all.